Drift and Swerve

November 2011
Spokane

Drift and Swerve

Samuel Ligon

To EJ

It was great
meeting you at
Gonzaga   Cheers!

Autumn House Press

PITTSBURGH

Autumn House Press Staff
Executive Editor and Founder: Michael Simms
Executive Director: Richard St. John
Community Outreach Director: Michael Wurster
Co-Director: Eva-Maria Simms
Fiction Editor: Sharon Dilworth
Coal Hill Editor: Joshua Storey
Associate Editors: Anna Catone, Laurie Mansell Reich, Rebecca Clever, Philip Terman
Assistant Editor: Bernadette James
Editorial Consultant: Ziggy Edwards
Media Consultant: Jan Beatty
Tech Crew Chief: Michael Milberger
Interns: Carolyne Whelan, Laura Vrcek

ISBN: 978-1-932870-29-9

For Jane and Paul

Acknowledgments

Some of these stories first appeared in slightly different form in the following publications: *Alaska Quarterly Review*, "Drift and Swerve"; *Post Road*, "Animal Hater"; *The Empty Page: Fiction Inspired by* Sonic Youth, "Dirty Boots"; *Gulf Coast*, "Germans"; *The New Orleans Review*, "Something Awful"; *Art Savant*, "Heavy Bag"; *The Flash*,"Glazed"; *Manoa*, "Arson" (under the title "Graceland"); *Keyhole*, "Cleavage"; *Sleepingfish*, "American League."

For editorial suggestions, I would like to thank Robert Lopez, Christopher Chambers, Joseph Salvatore, Paul Agostino, Derek White, William Walsh, Brian Mandabach, Shawn Vestal, and Sharon Dilworth.

Contents

Providence

Nikki doesn't know how much longer she can wait around for this Buckley, Nikki not knowing if that's his first name or last, just Buckley, supposed to be here fifteen minutes ago, Nikki perched on a brick wall off Wickenden waiting. Frank would kill her if he knew—just a little weed and he'd go bullshit on her—but that's the way with Frank since he landed in the hospital last month after a beating outside Babe's, and quit everything cold turkey the next day. Now he wants her to quit everything too. She thought he was weak when he was drinking, Frank, but it's when he stopped that the weakness really took hold. Or, no, not weakness. More like deadness.

At 3:30 she is definitely going to leave—walk home and get changed before heading to La Chatte du Maison, a lesbian bistro off Hope Street where Nikki pearl dives, what La Femme Danielle, the owner of La Chatte, calls dishwashing. Nikki doesn't mind the lesbian flirting, the jokes about pearl diving and house pussy, because no one there cares if she's stoned or finishes drinks, as long as she does her job, which is much more bearable stoned. But in five minutes she will have to leave, weed or no weed, fuck this Buckley. And Frank. And everyone in this town. All she can show for six months in Providence is fifteen twenty-dollar bills stashed in her backpack, and she hardly spends money on food as it is, eating at The Pussy when she works, stealing as much from the walk-in as she can manage, but it's never enough. She's always hungry. If she had a thousand bucks she'd go someplace cheap and warm, Florida maybe, if that is cheap and warm. She could work with kids probably, in a pre-school or daycare, like her cousin Melanie used to do. Or she could go to college.

A dude rounds the corner from Wickenden, dressed in board shorts and expensive sandals, his bleached straw hair in his eyes, saying, "You Nikki?"

He opens a gate in the brick wall. "I'm Bradley."

She drops to the sidewalk. "Buckley?" she says, and he says, "Come on," and she follows him across a concrete patio.

Inside, he unlocks the door to number 4. "I'm not late, am I?" he says, ushering her through his kitchen and into the living room, his backpack sliding off him onto the floor. "Just one second."

"You are late," she says, but he's already gone.

Nudes cover the walls, sloppy oils in reds and blacks. A mannequin by the window looks toward the fuel tanks over in East Providence, most of her body day-glo except for her black Hitler mustache and bush—a magic marker fountain between her legs—copies of *Art in America* scattered around the paint-speckled floor at her feet. Buckley must be a RISD student. Nikki didn't always hate school—just the people, the teachers and students, the do-good-ers in the Upward Bound program back in New Hampshire always trying to save her from something, until they caught her when she was sixteen fucking in the summer dorm and sent her home. As if her mother cared. As if the world didn't depend upon the fertile fucking.

Buckley's stereo sits on a shelf over a long row of records, the cover to the new Throwing Muses album, *House Tornado*, facing out, that song, "Mexican Women," always sending a shiver through Nikki, Kristin Hersh's warbling voice a kind of frantic wailing—like she's about to rip herself out of her skin. And she can't be that much older than Nikki, that's the thing of it.

"You wanna beer?" Buckley calls, and Nikki says okay, and does he mind if she puts on *House Tornado* because she loves that album.

"Yeah," he says, "just a sec," meaning, she guesses, she's not allowed to touch the stereo. A two foot Graphics bong sits on the coffee table in front of her, a weed tray beside it empty except for seeds and stems and smears of ash.

Buckley walks in with two pints of Haffenreffer, drops the needle on *House Tornado*, then opens a closet door and pulls down a black shoeshine box.

Nikki holds up her sneakered foot. "You can try to shine these," she says.

Buckley grins as he unlatches a side door on the box. He takes out five or six quarter bags and lays them on the coffee table by the bong. "Take your pick," he says.

Kristin Hersh sings, "I'm losing my friends."

Nikki doesn't think she has friends anymore. Not real ones anyway. Not the kind that hold secrets. If she does have them, they're up in New Hampshire finishing high school, consuming themselves with plans for senior week, for summer and college. Less than two hundred miles away, they might as well be dead.

Buckley dumps a bag on the tray and starts loading a six hit slider.

Nikki's got five minutes if she wants to change before work. At least Frank won't be home to smell her.

"Tina said you work at La Chatte," Buckley says, handing her the bong and a lighter. "You go to Brown?"

Nikki knows she can't be confused with a Brown student. She has the wrong clothes, the wrong hair. The wrong everything. "Yeah, right," she says. She takes a huge hit and holds it. "I hate those fuckers."

Buckley laughs. "RISD students too," he says, referring to the snotty art school.

Nikki blows her hit toward the mannequin by the window.

"I've only got one year left," he says. "But I might not finish."

Nikki doesn't prompt him. She drinks her beer while Buckley hits the bong. If she could have the money he's not going to spend on RISD tuition, she'd buy a car and visit every place she's ever heard of until the money ran out. She examines the bags of weed, takes the biggest, and hands Buckley three twenties. "Those paintings are pretty cool," she says, nodding toward the nudes.

"You like them?"

"The middle one," Nikki says. "That girl looks crazy."

Buckley stands and takes the painting from the wall. "Take it," he says, propping the canvas on the couch next to her.

Nikki wonders if Buckley painted the girl and then fucked her—if giving the painting to Nikki takes something away from that girl, makes her cheap. She knows the painting really has nothing to do with the girl, which is even worse. Or maybe not. It looks like Buckley was afraid of her, with her proud, defiant eyes, a sort of glare.

"What's her name?" Nikki says.

Buckley shrugs. "She was a model," he says. "At school."

"You don't know her name?"

"I couldn't get her left foot right," he says, pointing to the canvas.

This close her foot looks like red-streaked putty, a moss-covered rock.

Nikki looks at the girl in the painting, a nude model without a name, her eyes sort of flat and dead. Nikki could do that—take off her clothes and lie on a blanket while painters turned her body into rock. Especially if she could pick the music.

"You want it?" Buckley says. "Take it."

A buzzer sounds somewhere in the apartment. Buckley walks through the kitchen and out the door to the back hall. He's different than she thought he would be, though everyone is, until they become their predictable, moronic selves. She hears voices from the hall, then Buckley leads another guy into the room, a dude she knew for three days six months ago, after she lost George when she first got to Providence. Met him on Thayer Street in the middle of October with no money and no place to stay. Stole a big fisherman's sweater from his closet.

"Nikki, this is Pierce," Buckley says, and Nikki, standing, says, "I know Pierce," and Pierce says, "Hey, Nikki," and Nikki says, "I gotta go. Thanks, man," and Buckley picks up the painting from the couch and says, "Don't forget this," and Nikki says, "Are you sure?" looking at the painting, trying to decide if she really does like it, if she could even love it, because, otherwise, she's not taking it, she's not that cold—to drop a dude's painting in a dumpster on her way home—but Buckley's pushing it toward her before she can decide, then walking her through the kitchen, saying, "You wanna get a beer sometime? Coffee?" Nikki nodding, like, maybe, and Buckley rummages through a junk drawer, pulls out a pen and yellow legal pad, and asks for her number.

"I don't have a phone," Nikki says.

"Thanks for this," she says, holding up the painting, and then she's out and away.

At home, even though she's late for work, Nikki rolls a joint, smokes half, and puts the roach in a cellophane in her jeans pocket for later. She hides the painting in the shared basement of the six-unit building, the fucked-up girl's face against the wall. If Frank saw it, he'd go bullshit on her: "Where'd you get that? Dude just wants to get in your pants." She runs upstairs for a sheet to wrap the painting in, wondering if she'll take it with her when she goes, or if someone will discover it years from now and hang it in their dingy little living room upstairs. Maybe she should look at it one more time, in case she never comes back, but she's too late for that. If she walks slow enough, she can smoke a whole cigarette before reaching the alley door to The Pussy's kitchen.

"Put that out and get in here," La Femme Danielle says, pushing open the screen. "It's almost five o'clock. Come on, come on, get in here."

Already both sinks and the back table are overloaded with pots and pans and trays from the lunch steam table.

"What the fuck," Nikki says, and Danielle says, "I'll make it up to you."

"How?" Nikki says, tying her apron strings around her waist.

Danielle breezes through the kitchen and out the swinging door to the dining room. And to make matters worse, Ilsa's working.

"Where's Slater?" Nikki calls, and Becky, one of the line cooks, says, "Sick."

Ilsa steps into the back room on her way to the walk-in. "No fucking off," she says. "And I mean it, Nikki."

"Oh, please," Nikki says.

Ilsa cooking means no music in the kitchen, or worse, easy listening. Nikki unloads dishes from the soak sink, stacks them on the table behind her that's piled with crusted pans. She's either too high or not high enough, but no way can she make this shift without music. She unties her apron, hangs it on a steel plate rack, then sticks her head in the kitchen proper and says to Becky, "I'll be right back. I forgot my tunes."

"Absolutely not," Ilsa says coming back from the walk-in.

"It'll just take a sec," Nikki says, and Ilsa says, "No," and Nikki says, "Yes," and Ilsa's fair skin under her netted blond curls goes pink, the last thing Nikki sees before bolting through the screen door.

But she forgot about Frank. Now that he doesn't drink he's home all the time, and walking east on Transit, she sees his van parked on the street. They haven't really talked lately, haven't seen each other, Frank delivering couches for Castro Convertibles all day and Nikki pearl diving four nights a week, and now that the weather's getting nice, staying away when she's not working, walking. She met him at a Max Creek show at Lupo's five months ago, came home with him and never left. At 35, he's three years younger than her mother, but now with the nagging, making Nikki smoke outside, sniffing around her all the time, he acts more like 50. Without the drinking, without weed, without Percocets or acid or even cigarettes, he never wants to do anything but watch TV. Three nights ago, to make up for the not talking, her smoking and drinking and not knowing how to cook, and hopefully, to keep him from saying what she knows he's been thinking, she sucked him off while he watched The Cosby Show and she listened to Dinosaur Jr. through her headphones. Sometimes in the morning he fucks her before work, but she pretty much sleeps through it. They never fuck at night anymore.

And he's not such a bad guy. They had some fun together those first few months, but then he landed in the hospital and came out wanting her to change. And there's never any music in the house, just the noise of the TV floating back to the kitchen table, where, if she's not out, she works crossword puzzles from a book, waiting for him to go to bed, wondering when he'll kick her out and what she'll do then.

She can hear the goddamn thing blasting from out in the hallway. She needs to get in quick, pick up her Walkman, the new Dinosaur Jr. tape, *BUG*, still in there, and get back to The Pussy before Danielle decides to fire her.

But he's not in the living room when she walks in, not in the kitchen. The TV's blasting city news, a fire raging in Pawtucket, and he's not in the bathroom either. Where he is is on his bed, the contents of her backpack spread around him, her tapes, her Walkman, her paraphernalia pouch, a couple books, his face inside her new bag of weed, smelling, his eyes watching her over the plastic as if he's not surprised to see her.

He squints at her as he breathes in the smell of the weed.

"Give me that," Nikki says.

He looks at the weed in his hand, at Nikki. He's chewing gum.

"Right now."

"Shut up, Nikki."

He sticks his face in the bag, then lowers it and picks up her backpack.

Nikki says, "Don't," and Frank says, "I come home from work and there's clouds in the kitchen?" He shakes her empty backpack upside down over the bed. "How you think that makes me feel, Nikki? Jonesing in my own house."

He tosses the pack toward her. "You got money for weed, but not for nothing else, right?"

She gathers her belongings from the bed and jams them into her pack, the money sock missing.

"I only took what's coming to me," Frank says, tossing her the sock, and, inside—she counts them fast—seven twenties. Eight missing.

"Give me my money, Frank," she says.

"I'm not even gonna bust balls on food," he says, sticking his face in her bag of weed again. "Or late rent, the tiny bit you pay."

"Right now," she says, and he says, "That ain't half the heat or electric since you been here."

"You never asked for electric," she says. "Give me my fucking money."

She grabs for the weed, but Frank jerks his hand away, dangling the bag in the air.

In third grade, Tommy Jessup caught lethargic flies on their classroom window ledge and leashed them with strands of hair pulled from Nikki's head. They'd buzz drunkenly on the leash for awhile, then Tommy would take off their legs. One day during independent reading, Tommy's face close to his desk as he removed a fly's leg, Nikki came back from the book corner with a dictionary and slammed it against the fucker's head, chipping three teeth.

Now, she folds her arms across her chest, waiting for Frank to hand over her money. He watches her with his pointed rat's face, still dangling the bag by his ear, then drops the weed to the bed. A minute passes. They look at each other. "You think I'm a complete asshole?" he says. "Like you?"

Nikki picks up the weed, jams it in her pocket.

"You think I got money put away?"

He stands from the bed, Nikki following him to the kitchen. Most of her clothes are in milk crates next to the closet, plus a winter coat, a pillow, and a few other things scattered around. But she's got her good leather backpack, her weed, her Walkman and most of her tapes. And less than half her money.

He opens drawers in the kitchen, cabinets. "Where's it at, Nikki?" he says. "Where am I hiding it?" He reaches into the cabinet above the stove, sweeping macaroni and cereal to the floor. "I help you all this time and you got money on the side? Where's my savings?"

He dumps the silverware drawer into the stink, stands looking at forks and knives, a ladle, a spatula.

Nikki looks into the sink with him. "You'd pay three hundred a month whether I'm here or not," she says.

"Jesus, Nikki," Frank says. "You have no fucking idea what I'm talking about."

"So what are you talking about?"

"What's fucking fair."

"Like stealing my money?"

"Like you not paying when you could? Hiding shit. Making me pay. For fucking everything?" He reaches into his tee shirt pocket, jerks out the money and hands it to her. "Here you go, Nikki," he says. "Get out."

She touch-counts the eight bills, watching his face. "I'm sorry, Frank," she says. "I am. But you shouldn't go through my stuff."

"I was looking for the fucking weed," he says. "I was gonna roll one."

"Maybe you should have," she says, reaching for his hand.

"Just go," he says.

She could blow him right here in the kitchen, buy a week, two weeks. A month? She reaches for his belt, but he swats her hand away and walks out to his couch and television.

"Frank," she says, holding up the Walkman, "I just came for this."

"I wasn't hiding that money," she says.

"Get out."

"I gotta work," she says. "Frank. Please."

He concentrates on the television, and the worst of it is that this might be the nicest he's been to her in weeks, not hitting her even now, when she so clearly deserves it, proving finally that there's no chance to make things right and keep her cheap place to live, proving that he is done with her once and for all, not that she'll miss him in any way, but how is she going to save escape money now when she won't even have enough to live in Providence?

She races back to The Pussy with her Walkman and tapes and books and weed, her three hundred dollars, two hundred ninety more than when George disappeared and she didn't know one person in this town. That was fall, six months ago, Nikki walking Thayer Street looking for him, panhandling in front of CVS, certain he would show up simply because she loved him. Because he loved her, because it was love at first sight at Short Sands Beach on a Saturday afternoon in August with Crystal and Jenn, when she had been looking for nothing and found him and still expected nothing until a week later when he tracked her all the way back to Manchester, showed up at her mother's house and took her away, camping Downeast Maine until the money ran out a few weeks later, then on to Providence where he had a cousin, an uncle, someone who owed him money, the possibility of a job, where he left her, the memory of George always making Nikki hate herself, to be such a little girl in love waiting for a boy who would never return. Left her with ten dollars on the street, and when she thinks about it that way, she realizes that, now, with three hundred dollars, she's actually in pretty good shape. Practically rich. But she can't think about it that way. Not really. She feels herself sinking deeper into stuck, and back at The Pussy, La Femme Danielle is elbows deep at the sinks, twisting to meet Nikki's eyes when the screen slams, and though she'll ultimately be pissed and maybe still fire Nikki, right now she is only relieved, saying, "Oh thank God you're here," and Nikki, already pulling an apron over her head, says, "I'm sorry—I'm—my boyfriend," such a ridiculous word to describe Frank, and she thinks she might even be able to bring up a tear or two, saying, "He's, we're, I'm—"

"Shh," Danielle says, untying her apron, then taking Nikki in her arms.

"I'm sorry, baby," she whispers in Nikki's ear. "I want to hear about it. I do. But we're getting slammed out there. I want to hear all about it over a glass of wine later. Okay?"

Nikki nods. She's relieved for a minute, watching Danielle make her way back to the front of the restaurant where she belongs, then horrified. What the fuck is she supposed to do now?

Five hours later she can't tell the difference between her sweat and the dishwater soaking her pants, her apron, her T-shirt, her socks, her underwear, the skin of her hands, half way up her forearms, pale and shriveled and dead, soft enough to slough off with a butter knife, and throughout the night, instead of taking a break, she runs the water hotter in her sinks as the tape loops on her Walkman, that song "Don't" like the soundtrack to a horror movie, the partially buried nearly satanic shrieking under wailing guitars— "Why?" he shrieks, but until tonight Nikki has heard the rest wrong, hearing his distorted howling as "Why don't you fuck me?" or, sometimes, "Why don't you bite me?" when in fact, under all the psychedelic noise, he's saying, "Why don't you like me?" which seems much worse, somehow, especially when Nikki considers her mother, the men she would bring home from time to time, but who never liked her because she was unlikable, though that's not what makes Nikki add more hot water to the sink and turn the volume up until the music burns her eyes. The bad part is the immediate past, reaching for Frank's belt in his kitchen in hopes of another week at his place, which puts the value of the act at, what? twenty bucks? And how weird it is that she'd be willing to lay down nude on a blanket for Buckley to paint but won't consider applying for a job at the Foxy Lady, which she knows goddamn good and well would make her rich, but which would also get her deeper stuck in something she can't quite name or understand, her mother's mastectomies ending that problem for her once and for all, and taking far more away, it seemed to Nikki, than her tits, because her mother was so goddamn vain, so aware of her beauty, her body, to the exclusion of everything else, her body being finally the only thing she cared about, and while it's one thing to like sex, to know your body, to take pleasure in pleasure, shit, to understand the real power it gives you, it's another thing to invest everything in the body, to earn a living from the body, making the weight of it almost too much to bear, and the ultimate betrayal, when the body begins its sag and collapse—in what? five years? eight years? ten? work out all you want, but it's going to happen—that much harder to take. But she won't be a slave to other people's ideas about it, either. She's not a whore. And what if she was? Whose fucking business is that?

The thing you have to figure out first is where, not what. And certainly not who.

Becky scares the shit out of Nikki, tapping her shoulder and offering a glass of wine. Nikki turns off the Walkman under her apron, wipes her hands and pulls the headphones from her ears. "There's a guy at the bar asking for you," Becky says, bringing on the old jolt, the old lie, and Nikki wonders how much more time she can waste hating George, waiting for George, loving George.

Fucking George.

She puts the wine glass on the nearly empty table behind her, thanks Becky, who goes back to scouring the grill. There's almost nothing left to wash, one bus pan, two big pots, a few trays from the steam table. "Pretty cute, too," Becky says, "if you like that kind of thing."

The door from the dining room swings open, La Femme Danielle leading one of her beautiful girlfriends into the kitchen toward the office in back, both of them flushed from whatever they've been drinking. "Nikki, Nikki," La Femme says, "leave the rest to soak and bring your wine back to the office for a treat. Nikki has boy trouble," she says to her companion, who tilts her head and plays with her hair.

"Poor thing," the friend says, reaching a manicured hand toward Nikki's face.

Nikki jerks her head.

"Ooooh," the friend says, "I wasn't going to hurt you. I was just—" and she reaches again for Nikki, who this time allows her to push a strand of hair behind her ear.

"You just look so sweaty," she says. "I'm Erica."

"Nikki," Nikki says.

"Take off your bib and come back for some candy," Erica says, following La Femme out of the room.

Nikki clears the back table, gulps her wine. "What's he look like?" she says to Becky, who's folding the floor mats so she can mop under them.

"Sort of shaggy," Becky says.

"Shaggy?" Nikki says. None of them has seen Frank. And, after all this time, George wouldn't know where to find her, wouldn't care to find her, anyway. It is pathetic that she has to remind herself of this, after the way he bailed on her, though a part of her still wonders, still hopes in a sick way that something horrible happened to him—that he was abducted, murdered, beaten until he lost his memory, anything to explain his sudden absence as something other than a complete blow-off when Nikki was broke and without one contact in this town. The place he brought her.

Nikki drops her apron in the laundry bag. She's played this scene in her mind before, George coming back to her begging forgiveness, and Nikki spitting on him or slapping his face, until, finally, after he explains the agony of his months held hostage, she agrees to take him back.

But it's Buckley at the bar, of course, not George. George is still dead, still lost in the wilderness, and she's glad of it. But what to say to this Buckley?

She'll have to say something, if she wants to crash at his place for the next couple nights or weeks or months—until she has enough money to get out of Providence. Buckley sitting at the bar is proof of something. She can fit everything she owns in a garbage bag, and Buckley can carry his own painting back to his apartment off Wickenden.

But she's soaking wet still, her limp hair stinking of the kitchen.

She sneaks out of the dining room and back to the office, where La Femme Danielle sits behind her desk. Erica stands opposite her, bent over a mirror she holds in her hand, snorting two long rails before passing the mirror and straw to Nikki.

"Don't do that to me again now, Nikki," La Femme says. "Come in late and leave and scare me half to death."

Nikki finishes her first line and tilts her head for the drip. "No," she says. "I was having—"

"I know," La Femme says, "I know."

"Boy trouble," Erica says, and she reaches out and pinches Nikki's right nipple.

Nikki drops the mirror. She means to slap Erica's hand away but ends up backhanding her in the nose, Erica saying, "Oh, shit," and dropping her face in her hands.

"Don't fucking touch me," Nikki says, a little surprised by the sound of her voice in this room, the power of it.

"It's bleeding," Erica whines, pinching her nose between both hands as if praying.

"Nikki," La Femme says, standing, "go get a broom," and Nikki looks at her, looks at Erica holding her nose.

La Femme snaps her fingers, points toward the door. "Get the broom, Nikki—if you want another treat."

Nikki sees herself a fat, tattooed, forty-five year old woman, curled at the feet of an even fatter, powdered Femme Danielle, being offered chicken legs and lines of coke and buckets of wine, and she says, "I need money."

"Money?" La Femme says, and Erica says, "Don't we all," and Nikki says, "I need eight hundred bucks," and La Femme says, "Payday's next Friday," and Nikki says, "I have to find a new place tonight."

"Get the broom, Nikki," Erica says, and Nikki says, "Fuck off, Erica," and La Femme says, "Do you want to be out on your ass?"

"I need money."

La Femme stands over her desk, pointing toward the door. "Get the broom, Nikki," she says. "Right fucking now."

Much later, hours and days and months and two joints and a hit of ex later, Nikki and Buckley are the stars of a Brown party off Thayer Street, and the amazing thing is that time hasn't begun its rapid acceleration yet after all. She sits on Buckley's lap as he runs his hand up and down her back, through her hair and around her neck, his other arm lying across her legs and she sees by his watch that it's not yet one o'clock. Newcomers pour into the kitchen for beer, the Talking Heads from ten years ago blasting over warped floorboards in the living room, through French doors to a little deck sagging over Benevolent Street, and it's as if she and Buckley have been together forever but that the newness of their attraction hasn't worn off. Everyone knows Buckley and wants to know her. How clever she is and how beautiful. Walking back to Frank's place from La Chatte, after storming out of La Femme's office and through the restaurant, and then the bar, where she feigned surprise at seeing Buckley, who said her name and followed her out the front door and around the corner to Transit Street, Nikki had the strangest feeling that Frank would be dead in the bathtub, OD'd or his veins opened in the now cold water, but not only was Frank not dead, he wasn't even there. And then, to make everything better, after she gathered her belongings in a garbage bag and directed Buckley downstairs to get the painting, as she was making one last sweep of the apartment, Frank showed up with a pint of ice cream, still not dead. They even hugged goodbye, Buckley smart enough to read the situation from the hallway and wait outside unseen. And to make matters better still, she showered at Buckley's place so that now there is no stink of La Chatte on her whatsoever. Everything she owns is gathered and safe at Buckley's.

The ex starts to take effect, warm butter running through her arms and legs, spinning in her stomach. She needs to stretch and get another beer and talk to these excellent people and dance in the living room, where this one chick—maybe half-black or a quarter or less, what her mother called an octoroon, such a horrible, nasty word, and this is the kind of filth Nikki has to purge herself of, to look at the girl with her beautiful face and long braided hair and have the word "octoroon" come into her mind is a perfect example of the poison her mother raised her on, that song "Artists Only" blasting and the girl starting to pogo, so that Nikki has to do it too, Buckley holding the beers as Nikki pogos in circles around the beautiful, sweaty girl, her eyes blazing—everybody's on ex—the beautiful girl offering Nikki her hands so they can spin as they pogo, the center of the dance. And they keep spinning and dancing as the songs change, one into another, taking drinks of beer and water and wine Buckley or other people provide, Buckley there dancing, too, and that guy Pierce, and it's like she knows all these fine, good people, has always known them, will always know them, the beautiful girl coming in close, rubbing her body against Nikki, sort of shimmering against her, her mouth close to Nikki's ear, breathing and licking, and she says, "I'm Maya," and Nikki shimmies back against her, touches the spot behind her jawbone under her earlobe with the tip of her tongue and says her name, "Nikki." She's never fucked around with a girl before but this chick is so hot, and plus, really, she just loves everyone. An excellent song she doesn't know comes on and Maya sort of humps herself against Nikki's leg, not in a crude way, just real liquidy, and then she's got the bottom of Nikki's shirt in her hands, pulling Nikki toward her and they start to kiss, Maya's mouth and tongue so warm and sweet it all seems perfectly natural, so good and right, Buckley's big face suddenly part of it, too, and then she's kissing him, facing him, Maya behind rubbing her hands over Nikki's breasts and back down into the front of her jeans and back over her breasts as she kisses Buckley, and it's like, why can't they just take off their clothes right here on the dance floor? She pulls away from Buckley for a minute to breathe, turns her head as they continue to dance or whatever it is they're doing, Maya's arms still wrapped around her, and Pierce's sweaty face is there, Pierce's mouth, his tongue and this look in his eyes like he's starving to death, a fucking rodent attaching himself to Nikki's face, her mouth, all of it happening so fast in the blur of the music and ex—she pushes him away with a flat hand to the side of his face so hard he crashes into Buckley before spinning off and landing on the floor.

Nikki just wants to spit the taste of his tongue out of her mouth.

Maya's like, "Are you okay?" and Buckley screams, "What happened?" and Nikki says, "I have to get some air," Pierce pulling himself from the floor and fixing Nikki with pure hate in his animal eyes.

"Fuck you," she screams at him.

Buckley spins around. "What are you doing, man?"

Pierce holds up his hands. "Dude, nothing, man." And the crowd swallows him.

Beer is what she needs. Beer and air and cigarettes. The little balcony tilted over Benevolent Street is empty, the bodies all on the dance floor. Nikki stands against the railing, looking down at the drunk stoned students wandering below. Buckley appears beside her with a cup of water. She drinks it down and hands him the cup. "What happened?" he says. "I didn't see—"

"Could you get us beer?" Nikki says.

She sits on a rusty chair breathing. It might be cold out. She might be freezing.

"Don't touch her," Maya says, and when Nikki jerks her head, Pierce is behind her pulling his hands back to himself. Maya stands farther back, all shadow in the backlight from the living room. "Get out," Maya says. "You fuck."

Pierce growls something, but slinks back to the throbbing living room, and Maya says, "Fucking pig," as she slides an empty keg next to Nikki for a chair. They're quiet a few minutes, the floor lurching under them with the bouncing from the living room, and it seems likely the deck will fall off the side of the building and pitch its contents down to the street below, not far enough to kill them probably, but who knows? Nikki's cigarette seems to smoke itself, and Maya's been talking for some time, weaving her voice into the music, planting names of people Nikki's never heard of into the night, Bodeyair, Nin, Wolf, Dorkin, saying, "I was three rows behind you at Schuler's lecture, but on the other side of the room," and Nikki says, "Schuler?"

"That idea of the cloistered feminist," Maya says, "the quiet revolutionary—like a stealth attack—"

Nikki doesn't try to follow; she lets herself get lost in the river of Maya's words.

A cup of beer appears in front of her attached to Buckley's hand. Even though she's wide awake, still buzzing with the ex, she's too tired to keep up anymore. She wishes they would just fuck her and be done with her. Let her sit on a couch in an empty place, Buckley's living room with the Hitler mannequin, let her use the stereo, the bong. "Let's do another hit," she says, interrupting them. She looks at Maya. She looks at Buckley. "Let's do another hit somewhere else."

Back in Buckley's living room off Wickenden, Nikki rehangs the nude while Buckley cuts the ex into three bumps because he and Maya agree that nobody needs another whole hit, Kristin Hersh on the turntable saying, "Keep walking," and a minute later, "Does love sit cold 'til you put it somewhere?" And later still, another song, she says, "I didn't care, I didn't care, I didn't care, I didn't care," and they talk and talk, Maya and Buckley, so that's good, that they have each other, and Nikki opens beers and loads bongs and chooses the music and participates in the conversation when she can, and gives Maya a back rub and gives Buckley a back rub and helps Maya out of her top because the ex is kicking hard, and then helps them back to Buckley's bed, loses herself a little in the fucking even, but not too much because she has to keep her senses about her now that she knows what's going to happen. There's a moment on the bed when Buckley looks at her, keeps looking at her, touching her face with his hand, a moment when they seem to see each other, study each other, Buckley staring into her eyes, rubbing her face with his fingertips, touching her hair, until Nikki finally takes his hand and redirects it to Maya's breast, Maya's ribs, Maya's belly, Maya's pussy, helping Buckley focus on this other body on the bed, and it seems to Nikki that these two have found each other, Maya and Buckley, that they're made for each other, so beautiful and smart, and that makes it so much easier, really, to do what she has to do. Not kill herself, she'd never do that. Just get one more chance. A chance of her own. No George. No Frank. No Femme. No Buckley. And so she wishes and wishes and hopes and hopes and maybe she does love this Maya a little, this Buckley, as they kiss and touch and lick and fuck, and she wishes and hopes that there will be enough for her of Buckley's, when added to her three hundred, to take her away. It's not the ex either, she hopes, that convinces her there will be enough. And it's kind of sad that the three of them can't be together like this forever. They're so kind to each other, so considerate, Maya bringing cold water, Buckley rubbing Nikki's feet, Nikki holding both of them while they fuck, then holding and lighting the bong for them, feeding them joints and beer to help them come down and sleep.

It occurs to her before she leaves the bed that it's better they've had no chance to reveal who they are to each other, that they've only made their best selves visible. That they'll always be perfect together.

She's so sure of her good luck she doesn't even panic when the shoe-shine box offers nothing but four bags of weed. So sure, she writes them a note at Buckley's kitchen counter before she finds the money, apologizing and promising to repay him and telling them both how much she loves them and how this isn't the ex talking, because it's seven-thirty in the morning, but that she really does love them more than she's ever loved anyone and that she always will and will never forget them or this night. She finds the money in a frozen juice cylinder in the freezer, a roll of hundreds and twenties, over two thousand bucks. Enough, she knows, to go south. Walking to the bus station with her good leather backpack and green garbage bag filled with everything else, Nikki thinks she might even change her name before she arrives wherever it is she's going. Catherine, maybe. Or Elizabeth. Some armored name suggesting power and a past. A name to have when she finally gets somewhere.

Drift and Swerve

The highway was two concrete slabs with a deep drainage ditch between and on either side the most god-awful eternity of corn and soy, soy and corn, maybe a cloud of pig stink to be driven through at seventy-five miles an hour, the windows down and the father smoking Camels and cigars and everybody filmed over with drying sweat and tired and full of their Stuckey's still. The mother pulled herself upright in her seat and looked at the father. "What?" the father said.

"You know what."

"I don't know what," the father said.

The tires fwapped over black goopy seams in the concrete.

"You know good and well she doesn't like it in the house," the mother said.

"Your brother brought it," the father said. "Not me."

"I don't care who brought it."

"Three beers apiece won't make her hate me more than she already does," the father said. "It's too late for that."

A buzz saw whine of cicadas came up over the road sounds, rose and fell away.

Nobody was on the highway hardly. The sky seemed colorless before night.

"Too late for what?" the sister said, and the mother said, "Are you eaves-dropping?" and the sister said, "No," and the brother said, "Yeah, you were," and the mother said, "Hush up, both of you," and the father said, "Go on to sleep; we won't be home 'til midnight."

"I'm not tired," the sister said, and then nobody said anything.

Sometime later, the brother spotted the drunk.

The vinyl seats were cooling, but the diesel stinking air was still heavy and hot.

The mother said, "Next time, I'll fly on ahead. You can drive the kids down later."

The father grunted, rubbed a yellowed handkerchief across the back of his neck.

"Maybe you can keep them at Jim's or Uncle Buddy's. It'll be worse next time."

"Look at that guy," the brother said, pointing over the front seat.

"I thought I told you to hush," the mother said.

The sister scooted to the center of the back seat and the brother pointed again. "See him?" he said.

Up ahead a car lurched and straightened, crept left, lurched right, and straightened.

The father said, "It'd be easier if she put the farm on the market now." He was unwrapping a cigar, then licking it all over. "Get a better price."

"You already got her in the ground, huh?"

He threw the balled up cellophane out the window.

"Litter bug," the sister whispered, and the brother hushed her.

"I'm just saying, you might take a bad price if you try to unload it quick. Grieving and all. Far away."

"Jim'll do all that."

"Uh-huh," the father said. "Might as well give it away."

"Maybe I just will," the mother said.

The father held up his index finger between them. "That son of a buck is drunk," he said, and the mother said, "Well maybe you shouldn't encourage it then," and the father bobbed his head toward the windshield until the mother saw it too. "Stay back, Boyd," she said, and he wrapped both hands around the wheel.

"That's what I was saying," the brother said.

"Drunk driver," the sister said.

The brother and sister leaned forward, their chins propped on the front seatback.

It was a blue Comet, one of the taillight lenses busted out and covered with red crepe paper, glowing pink.

"He's slowing down," the father said, and the mother said, "Well, keep back."

The Comet held straight in the right lane awhile, then drifted and lurched, weaving around the center lines.

"Drunk driver!" the sister shrieked.

"Yes, Emily," the mother said. "We know."

"Here comes somebody," the father said.

A truck was pulling up behind them, moving into the left lane to pass. The father pushed the lights off and pulled them back on three times. The truck kept gaining.

"Signal him," the mother said.

The father waved his hand out the window, pointing ahead. He flashed the lights again.

When the semi was about to overtake them, the father still waving and flashing, the oncoming diesel roar popped and deflated, and the truck drifted back, then pulled in behind them, winking his lights once.

"Yes!" the brother said.

The father rearranged himself in his seat, rolled his shoulders. He pushed himself back from the wheel until his arms were straight, then leaned back in.

"Do you think he saw all that flashing?" the mother said.

"Sure he did," the father said. "That's why he held back."

"Not him," the mother said. "The drunk."

The father shrugged.

"How could you get that drunk on a Sunday?" the mother said.

"Maybe he started on Friday."

"He could have a gun," the brother said.

"And you'd sure know about that, Boyd," the mother said.

The father tossed his cigar out the window and shook out a Camel.

"Look at him!" the sister said.

The Comet had dipped into the right shoulder, roostertailing dust and gravel, before pulling back onto the slab.

"Boyd, we've got to call the police," the mother said, and the brother and sister both said, "No!" and the brother said, "Who's gonna warn everyone?"

The lights from the truck behind flashed twice.

"Here comes another one," the father said.

They all looked back.

A big car, a Cadillac maybe, flew past the truck.

"Signal him," the mother said.

"I'll wave, Dad, you flash," the brother said.

The father flashed the lights three times.

"Get your hand in the car this instant," the mother said, but the brother ignored her.

The big car wasn't slowing.

"Signal him," the mother said, and the father kept flashing.

The Comet was only four or five car lengths ahead when the Cadillac flew by, honking as the Comet drifted toward him. Then he was past.

"What a foolish driver," the mother said. "Now back off, Boyd. And you, mister," she said, turning in her seat, "keep your hands in the car."

The truck was falling farther back so that the only illumination inside the car was the green glow from the dash and the Comet's taillights. They were back up to sixty-five, seventy, the Comet holding steady in the right lane.

"That one scared him," the mother said. "He had to see."

The sister pushed herself into the corner of the seat and leaned her head against the door. "Gramma told me Persia couldn't go to heaven because he doesn't have an internal soul," she said.

"That's not true," the brother said. "Dad."

"Sure it's true," the mother said.

"She said I could have him though. When she dies."

"No cats," the father said, and the mother said, "We'll see."

"She says a lot of stupid things," the brother said, and the mother turned and cuffed him over the eye and nose with the back of an open hand.

"What?" he said.

"All right," the father said. "Come on. I have to concentrate."

"Well, she does," the brother said, and the mother turned in her seat, poised to slap.

The brother held his hands up in front of him. "Like about men going to hell," he said, "boys becoming barnyard animals, horse-donged, and then going to hell."

The father shook his head and said, "That's what I've been saying," and the sister said, "Is that true?"

"Kevin," the mother said. She worked her palm under his chin and forced his face up. "You know that's not true, don't you?"

The brother nodded. "She's looking at me," he said.

"Emily," the mother said, "don't look at your brother."

"Do you know how foolish and sad that is?" the mother said, and the brother said, "That's what I mean about her saying stupid things."

"That's right," the father said.

"With all her pain," the mother said, "she's a little mean right now."

"Always has been," the father said.

The mother looked at the father, then back to the brother. "I'm sorry she said such a nasty thing to you."

"I don't care," the brother said, and the mother said, "Well, I do," and the sister said, "Maybe Gramma's going to hell now."

"Emily," the mother said, "you're asking for it," and the father said, "He's off the road!"

The mother turned in her seat.

The brother and sister leaned forward.

The front two wheels of the Comet threw gravel from the left shoulder, pulling the car toward the sloped concrete of the drainage ditch.

"Goddamn!" the father said, and the mother said, "Boyd!"

The Comet hit one of the aluminum reflector poles and another as it straightened out and the right front tire bumped up onto the slab, the back wheels fishtailing in the gravel before catching concrete.

Dust hung in a cloud behind the red and pink taillights, and the father said, "Speeding way up," and the mother said, "Catch him, Boyd," and the brother elbowed the sister in the ribs and she elbowed back, and he elbowed harder a few times until she started to cry.

"It was an accident," the brother said.

"Hush up," the mother said.

They were going eighty.

"Hand me a pack of smokes," the father said. "Open 'em up."

The mother reached into the glove compartment, pulled out a package of cigarettes and unwrapped them.

"Dickhead," the sister said.

"Emily Sue!" the mother said. She reached around to slap, but the sister was in the back corner of her seat so that the mother had to pull herself over the seatback to land one good shot to the sister's head.

Now she really cried.

The father bent over the wheel, his face close to the windshield.

"No one can hear you," the mother said.

"Hand me a cigarette," the father said.

The truck's lights were far behind them.

"Boyd, he's getting away," the mother said.

The sister whimpered.

The father leaned closer in to the windshield.

The brother pulled a pack of Juicy Fruit from his pocket, pushed it into the sister's lap. She slapped at his hand. "Take it," he whispered.

She took it and threw it on the floor at his feet. He picked it up and put it on the seat between them. "You can have it all," he whispered.

"You wanna talk about going to hell," the mother said.

They'd leveled off at eighty-five, were gaining.

"Where's the cops?" the mother said.

The father shook his head.

"I hate Gramma," the sister said, "always calling me split tail."

The mother's eyes were black and shiny in the green light as she turned and lifted herself over the seat. She grabbed the sister's outstretched arms by the wrists.

The sister winced, pulled back, and said, "I don't care. I do."

The mother held the sister's wrists in one hand and slapped the top of her head with the other, once, twice, the sister blubbering, "I don't care, I do," and the mother coming down on top of the sister's head again.

"Helen, Jesus," the father said. He held her by the sleeve of her blouse, then her shoulders, steering with his knee, and pulled her back to the front seat, saying, "Get ahold of yourself, Helen."

"Dirty little split tail she's always calling me," the sister cried, then pushed her face into the vinyl seat back.

The mother allowed herself to be encircled by the father's right arm, sunk into him. "Well, that's nothing new," she said.

The father tightened his hold. "Enough, Emily," he said.

The brother leaned his face into the wind pushing through his open window.

The mother straightened in her seat, stiff and still.

"Why do we always have to go?" the brother said.

The father opened and closed his hands on the wheel.

"Somebody has to take care of her," the mother said. She didn't look back. "You want her to die alone?"

"Hush now," the father said.

"Yes," the brother said into the wind.

The mother looked out her window.

The Comet straddled the white lines, getting away.

The father pushed it up to ninety.

"It's Jim being useless and me so far away," the mother said. "That's why."

The brother took off his sneakers, touched his sister's leg with his foot.

She slapped him away, stayed slouched in her corner.

The brother leaned over and said, "Watch," then crawled back to his side of the seat.

"Anybody'd be like that," the mother said.

He dangled his shoe out the window by the laces, looked to the sister, who was watching, and let it go.

"It's just a lot of things," the father said, hunched over the wheel.

The sister smiled.

The brother dropped his other shoe out the window.

"She wasn't always like that," the mother said. "You remember, Boyd."

The sister unstrapped her sandals.

"Sure," the father said.

She dropped both out the window at once.

The mother turned in her seat. "She wasn't always like that, kids. You remember don't you?"

"Yes," the brother said.

"Yes," the sister said.

"I'm sorry," the mother said, and the brother said, "It's okay."

The mother turned back around. "Remember that decoy she gave you, Boyd? You liked that."

"Sure I did," he said.

The Comet must have been going a hundred.

The sister reached under her skirt and pulled down her underpants. She held them out the window for a second waving like a flag, then let them go.

"Jesus," the father said, "what was that?" He craned his neck, squinting into the rearview mirror.

"What?" the mother said. "What was what?"

"Something flew by," the father said. "He's throwing things at us."

"It could be a UFO," the brother said.

There were other taillights ahead. The Comet had fallen into line.

"Or a ghost," the sister said.

As they approached the four-car line, the Comet lurched into the left lane and accelerated hard, then swerved back toward the second car in line.

A horn sounded.

"He's going to hit him!" the mother said.

The Comet jerked left and fell off the slab.

"Good lord!" the mother said.

"Crash!" the sister said.

The front left tire of the Comet bumped over the lip of the drainage ditch.

"Boyd!" the mother said.

The other tires followed.

The brother said, "Car crash!"

The Comet drove at an impossible angle along the concrete incline of the ditch, then slid down the wall on its wheels before tilting and toppling, the roof scraping along the floor, spouting a shower of orange sparks.

"Judas priest!" the mother said.

The father eased the station wagon into the left shoulder and they drove beside him, above him, the white and orange sparks ricocheting off either wall, the metal shrieking and groaning against the concrete.

The other cars had slowed as well.

The mother's door was open before the car stopped. "We've got to save him," she said, running toward the ditch.

"We saw him first," the brother said, opening his door.

The sister followed.

Other doors opened and closed.

The mother lost her footing on the mossy slime coating the drainage wall. She fell hard and slid down on her back.

The brother and sister sat and slid, the backs of their legs coated with slime.

The mother picked herself up and jogged bent over to the Comet, calling over her shoulder, "Bring a blanket, Boyd."

"Smoke on the Water" was playing, coming from inside the Comet.

"We'll call an ambulance," someone said up on the shoulder.

One of the front wheels was still turning, winding itself down.

"It could explode!" the brother shouted. He ran after the mother.

The sister wiped the goopy slime from the back of her legs, her bottom.

The drunk's arms appeared out the driver's window. His head and shoulders followed.

"Let me help you," the mother shouted over the music. She walked carefully along the incline, one hand against the Comet supporting her, then sat, or lay, her back against the slimy wall, her feet against the back door of the Comet. She offered her hand.

The drunk took it.

The brother and sister watched.

"Come on, now," the mother said, pulling him toward her. He had a scrape on his forehead, blood coming from his nose.

The father appeared with the car blanket. "Let me help," he said. He pushed the blanket at the brother, who dropped it.

But the drunk was most of the way out, only his legs still inside the car.

The mother held him against her, petting his crew cut.

"Fuck," he said.

"Shh," the mother said.

"Somebody's trying to kill me."

The father reached a hand toward them. "Here now," he said.

"It's okay," the mother said, petting him. "I've got you."

The brother said to the sister, "He's not going to die I bet."

"Come on," the father said, tapping the mother's shoulder and holding out his hand. "Let me help."

The drunk's blood was smeared over the mother's blouse.

"Some fuckin' Mexicans or something," the drunk said, "chasing me," and the mother said, "Let's not talk like that."

The drunk groaned, dropped his head against the mother's breast.

"Come on now," the father said. "Here."

"Probably not even hurt bad," the brother said.

With her big toe, the sister drew a circle in the slime, gave it two eyes and a smile.

"You can thank God we were here," the mother said.

The drunk tried to lift his head, but the mother pushed it back against her.

"Yeah," he said. "Thank God."

"Probably not Gramma either," the brother said. "Split tail."

The sister smiled, held up her skirt and spun.

"Watch this," the brother said. He ran away from her, away from the car and the mother and father, jumped, planted himself, and slid in the mossy slime.

The sister followed.

Barefooted, they ran and slid along the slippery concrete as if it were winter and the drainage ditch a frozen over river.

Animal Hater

Her husband is a cop. You see them once, after things have started, at The Glass Slipper, sitting around the big table in back with three or four other couples, cop friends, the men around him laughing like donkeys at whatever falls out of his mouth, and you would never guess, looking at them, that they are animal lovers.

Of course, she hates him.

Or maybe he's a broker or an insurance salesman.

She likes vodka and bad popular music and being shown off in the city. She likes to dance. At restaurants, before or after you go to bed, but usually before, she drinks wine and watches you shovel food into your mouth. When she hands you her plate, you eat what's left, a little of everything.

Her name is Michelle. You grope each other in cabs, kiss her hard on empty sidewalks.

You are always waiting to be killed.

Your wife's voice is preserved on the answering machine, instructing each caller to please leave a name, a number, and a brief message after the tone. There is no trace of insanity in this voice.

"What about Thursday?" Michelle might ask as you dress. "Can you get away?"

"I've been gone too much this week," you say, or, "Her parents are coming." You never mention Ellen's name.

Her husband's name is Don.

It has slipped a few times. Or John. He drives a Viper, was a boxer in the navy. He owns a construction firm. He is Greek or Italian or Black.

You wrap your hands around her throat as you kiss her, cutting the air, and she weaves her fingers into the roots of your hair, pulling. You roll off the bed, roll around the room, then pick her up and put her on the table, on a dresser, her eyes half back in her head like a dead woman's—but a dead woman who moves and makes noises.

Your daughter answers the phone when she calls. "Some lady's on the phone," she says. "Michelle."

"Who's that?" you say.

Carrie shrugs.

"I don't know any Michelles," you say.

The note from Ellen had read, "Take care of each other." A postcard from Denver said, "I'm sorry," and, "Evolution is painful."

You overhear Carrie say into the phone, "When are you coming home?" and, "Yes, he's cooking the meat."

Michelle has a stuffed cat the size of a fist attached to her key ring. On the street, she stops and pets the dogs of strangers. One afternoon she runs over a squirrel on the way to your daytime motel. She sits at the foot of the bed and cries. Whether this is an act or not doesn't matter. She won't let you touch her.

"Get away from me," she says when you try to comfort her.

You don't say that it was just a rodent.

"I should never drive," she says.

You knot your tie, put on your jacket.

She looks at you, standing in front of the mirror examining your work costume, then throws a shoe past your head.

"I've got a four o'clock meeting," you say.

"There's no such thing as a four o'clock meeting," she says.

"Marriage counseling," you say, and you leave her there. After five days apart, you wake with the taste of her skin in your mouth—salami and honeydew.

"You didn't say you had kids," she says. Carrie is at a friend's house, as she is every Friday night. "Just two," you say, "and another one on the way."

"We don't have any," Michelle says. "Don't want them." You order more drinks. "We have animals," she says.

You know this about her: that she has three dogs, a cat, four ferrets, and countless tropical fish. That she raises chickens in her suburban back yard.

At The Plaza, where she knows a manager who loans you a room, Michelle pulls nylons from her briefcase and instructs you as to how to tie her properly.

The knife is a dagger with mother of pearl and gold and semi-precious stones inlaid in the handle—suitably dramatic, but difficult to hold. The trick is in marking without going too deep. You run the point of the blade against the bottom of one foot, getting the feel for it, then up her calf and along the knee, over her thigh to her groin, and gently up around her belly button and under a breast, scraping nipple with the flat of the blade, up and down her neck, the knife standing, turning in a tiny point against her throat, then back down and over her topography.

Sometimes she flinches or strains toward the blade, pulling against the nylons holding her down. This is the dangerous part.

You feel like a sculptor, a surgeon.

You watch her grind her teeth and bite her lips. Before dressing, you notice a few dots of blood on her calf, and pink trails across her ribcage like tribal markings.

At the Bronx Zoo you keep track of the men who might be her husband, watching you, following you. There is a special exhibit called Butterflies—a gauzy, humidified tent filled with them, fluttering and threatening to become tangled in your hair. Carrie holds several up to her face on her index finger.

"Don't be afraid of them, Dad," she says. "They aren't going to hurt you."

"What about me hurting them?" you say. "If I panic."

"Dad," Carrie says.

There are repulsive cocoons in a display called Chrysalis Central, a few folded up butterflies emerging in the last section of the exhibit, the entire tranformative process laid out under glass.

After lunch you walk to Africa and see giraffes and zebras and antelope or gazelle, and on a hill far away, a pair of lions. It seems the lions might start slaughtering the zebras and gazelle. But nothing happens. In fact, they yawn a lot.

"Do you think they eat the zebras?" you ask Carrie.

"I think a truck goes in after the zoo closes, and a worker shovels them meat."

"Zebra meat?" you say.

"No," Carrie says. "Regular meat."

You move on to the elephants, watch them shift their enormous weight from foot to foot. "Your mother liked the zoo," you tell Carrie. "She could have told you about the animals." You remember Ellen teaching you how to ride a horse at her grandparents' farm, how patient she was, how careful not to make you feel like a fool.

"She's not dead," Carrie says.

"That's true," you say, wishing she were, and Carrie says, "These elephants stink."

You notice a man in a blue fishing hat who had earlier been in the butterfly tent, monitoring your movements. You consider introducing yourself and begging forgiveness, but decide it won't do any good.

Carrie cries on the phone in the kitchen. You eavesdrop from the living room. "But, why?" she asks. "What sacred path?"

In the corner near the ceiling, cobwebs move in a breeze you can't feel.

"You said it was temporary," Carrie says. "When will I see you?" She lowers her voice, then says, "I don't have another life," and hangs up the phone.

"Carrie," you call from your chair.

She sits at the kitchen table, her cheeks propped on fists, her face puffy and streaked.

"It's okay," you say, sitting beside her.

She flinches when you touch her hair.

"Your mother is very confused," you say. "It's not about you."

She swats your hand away. "Who's it about?" she says. "You?"

You shake your head. "Maybe," you say. "Partially," you say. "I don't really know." You sit together in the kitchen.

Eventually, Carrie leaves.

You wonder what kind of parent you have become, what kind of parent you ever were. What kind of husband.

You wonder—after Michelle tells you to hit her and you comply, if you are capable of this kind of violence.

"God," she says, breathing into your ear. "Jesus."

The sting resonates in the skin of your palm for days.

When Carrie was a toddler Ellen said it to her over and over: "We don't hit. We don't bite. You hurt Mommy. You hurt Daddy."

You wonder how a closed fist would feel against ribs beneath breasts—can feel the phantom crunch in the bones of your hand. We don't hit.

Except when all parties agree that it's best.

At the mall you buy Carrie whatever she wants, whatever she likes, shoes, a stuffed parrot, a book about insects. She's giddy with the rush of acquisition, then restrained, tentative.

"What about a coat?" you say. "A new jacket."

She shakes her head. "This is enough."

"That jacket looks ratty," you say. "You need a new one."

"It just needs to be washed."

"How sensible," you say. "How about something fun—a toy or a game."

"A toy?" she says, rolling her eyes.

At the Piercing Pagoda in the mall's main thoroughfare, Carrie models earrings in front of a mirror, trying on seductive predator faces she's seen on television. If you were to let go, you could vomit on the floor.

Instead, you say, "Those are nice."

"These?" Carrie says. "These are slutty."

"Oh," you say, certain she is too young to know that word. "Then by all means don't get them."

"Don't worry," she says. "I won't."

"Whichever ones you want," you say.

She wants none of them.

You have no idea what she does want.

At home, she stays with the television in her room.

Downstairs, you hold a book in your lap and wait to hit Michelle.

The phone rings three times, meaning Carrie must be asleep. The static and hum in the earpiece indicate that Ellen is still alive somewhere. "This is really childish," you finally say into the phone. "Really idiotic."

She waits.

"Carrie's not home," you say. "But, Ellen," and you pause dramatically: "She's doing very well without you. Much better than she did with you."

There's no click, just a dead or open line. She may or may not have heard you.

You turn off Carrie's television, wrap her blankets around her, touch her hair, imitating a mother, a parent.

That night you dream that Ellen gives birth to a goat. It occurs to you that insanity is probably contagious.

The next day, Michelle brings a blindfold and asks to be gagged.

The handcuffs are heavier than you'd imagined they'd be. "These first," she says. "You're a rapist. A terrorist-rapist."

"Did you get these from your husband?" you ask.

"Ron?" she says, or maybe "John?" or "Don?" or "Kahn?"

"These look real," you say.

"I got them at the Pink Pussycat," she says.

Michelle sits upright in the desk chair, waiting to be cuffed and gagged. Your body feels heavy; someone has turned up the gravity. "What are you waiting for?" she says.

You sit on the bed, facing her back. She watches you through the mirror. You're too tired for rape and terror. "I'm not sure what I'm supposed to do," you say, and she says, "Okay, we'll start after the initial struggle, once I'm restrained and subdued. Drugged possibly. You need to handcuff my ankles and wrists to the legs of the chair. Blindfold me. Gag me. And then start in, you know, doing stuff to me."

"Oh," you say, but you don't move.

An amount of time passes. You hear the shriek of laughter from an adjoining room. Your throat seems to be closing on itself. Michelle smiles at you, waiting. "Should I struggle?" she says, and you say, "How come you never hit me?"

She looks through the mirror, sizing you up. "You want me to hit you?" she says.

"Maybe," you say.

She won't stop looking at you.

"Go ahead," you say.

She stands, then sits beside you on the bed. She has no clothes on. You're wearing pleated pants and a T-shirt. She places a hand on your leg.

You see by her expression that you have become an injured animal, the squirrel she ran over on the expressway. The intimacy and tenderness are unbearable. She wraps her arms around you, pets your head against her shoulder.

You have no idea who she is or why she is doing this to you.

Perhaps you'll run into her someday down the road—at soccer practice or a recital—but it seems unlikely. In fact, you hope she dies in a car accident this very afternoon, then hate yourself for hoping it.

Eventually, she lets you go and gathers up the handcuffs, the gag, the blindfold.

"I'm okay," you say. "Don't worry about me.".

She fastens her skirt, adjusts her hair. "Good," she says. "I'm glad."

And then it's time to go back to work.

But you don't go back to work.

You park in the teacher's lot and make your way through school busses and screaming children. You have never been here before: it was Ellen who attended the parents' nights and teacher conferences, Ellen who made the cupcakes, Ellen who filled the house with things you will throw away.

Then you see Carrie, holding the hand of another girl and spinning as fast as they can, until the grip breaks and they fall to the lawn, laughing. You thought she was too old for this kind of behavior, this kind of play, but maybe she is not.

A woman in a pink suit and cotton candy hair approaches, not making eye contact, but unmistakably targeting you. "Can I help you?" she says. She smiles briefly, studies your face. Her walkie-talkie crackles in her hand. She probably knows everything.

Carrie is spinning again.

"Oh," you say, pointing. "That's my daughter."

She wants identification, which you fumble for and finally produce, all the while watching Carrie and the other girl spin, fall, laugh, and get up.

"I'll show you to the office," she says, and you say, "That's all right," and she says, "You can't be here without office clearance."

"I'm taking her home," you say, surprised by the parental authority in your voice.

"Not without clearance you're not," the official says.

You are aware that children around you are enjoying this minor confrontation between adults.

"Come with me," the woman says.

"I will," you say. "Just give me a minute."

Carrie and the other girl lock hands and spin. She hasn't seen you yet, and then, when she does, she jumps from the ground and runs toward you. "Dad!" she yells.

Thank you, you think, and you close your eyes.

Please, you think.

You must be praying.

"You'll still have to get clearance," the playground boss says.

And when you open your eyes, Carrie is running toward you, her face flushed with exertion. You crouch low, waiting, trying on faces of greeting, of comfort and reassurance, praying you'll find the face of recognition.

Vandals

A car rounds the corner at Whitmore Road, mid-size, Hugh decides, American-made, but moving at a respectable speed. Perched in his tree platform, Hugh imagines he can locate the driver's head through the foliage, sighting his .38 above the car's left headlight. Cinder blocks hang from branches, rigged to fall, and crates of railroad spikes wait to tip at the platform's edge. He almost told Roberta about the gun when he picked it up last month, as easy as laying down cash money and walking out with deadly force in a paper bag. Now, the way she's been whispering on the phone, afraid, he's glad she doesn't know.

Down the road the car slows and a searchlight beam pops onto Stokley's house.

Hugh's certain the vandals have acquired some high-tech equipment, then realizes it's the sheriff, coming around when he's no longer necessary— coming around at ten-thirty when the punks aren't done sniffing glue. The car picks up speed heading toward him, slows as it approaches, the searchlight sweeping his side yard, the static of the cop radio audible to Hugh fifteen feet above the LTD invisible. One cut of the nylon cord now and everything changes. The sheriff accelerates toward McCurdy's place, but Hugh still feels the rush of falling cinder blocks and railroad spikes—the joy of terror inside a car full of vandals. Then the back screen slams and Roberta calls, "Hugh? Telephone," as if he can just drop what he's doing and pick up the phone.

"It's your mother, honey," she says, walking around the side of the house. "Come down." He doesn't breathe, but she comes closer still, until she's right beneath the platform. "Something about Edna and Earl's anniversary," she says. "Just talk to her."

"I'm busy," Hugh whisper-spits. "Go on. You'll give me away."

"It's *your* mother," she says.

But he knows that Roberta called her. She's been trying to get everyone involved, trying to get him to just calm down. He'll calm down, all right, once they leave him alone. He's heard her on the phone with her friends and sister, making him out to be crazy, when he's only doing the most natural thing he can imagine.

The backdoor slams. He puts the gun away, takes out a pack of cigarettes from under the front corner of the futon, something else Roberta wouldn't understand. He's spent ten nights smoking and drinking coffee in the Command Post, but if the punks don't come in the next two nights, he'll have to figure out a way to sleep, a way to get up and go back to work when there's still so much work here.

The first attack—a single egg—didn't come until they were six months settled into the place, back when Hugh couldn't wait to get home at night, the hour commute an escape from the sprawl of stripmalls and subdivisions. He cleaned the egg off the front door and forgot about it. The mailbox got hit a month later, and Hugh was the first to say, "Just kids." Hadn't he been involved in his share of teenage vandalism—toilet paper and smashed pumpkins? But after three months of upended garbage cans and more than a dozen eggings, it was the sheriff who said, "Just kids looking for a reaction, Mr. Sinclair. Don't give them the satisfaction." Hugh chose to believe him—that it would all blow over if he ignored the vandals—until he and Roberta came home one night to deep doughnut ruts all over the side yard, his headlights illuminating what appeared to be an enormous woodchuck network.

"It's just those kids, again," Roberta said. But he heard the trembling in her voice, the frustration and helplessness. He started watching for them. Always. Started worrying he'd fall asleep during his commute. When the second mailbox got hit, he ran outside with a baseball bat and saw what looked like an old Ford wagon roaring away. But it was the destruction of the last mailbox—with dynamite—that revealed just how dangerous these animals could be. He had no intention of waiting for them to firebomb his house. To kill his family. It was a relief to finally be fully a part of the action. He can see them all laughing about it years from now over a beer, the boys regarding him as someone who'd dished out a hard but valuable lesson. You don't want to hurt them, he thinks, not really, don't want to kill them—

The back screen jangles. Could she possibly be coming out again, after all the instructions he's given? Steps crunch gravel back toward the shed. Then he sees her at the corner of the house, her white bathrobe fluorescent in the moonlight.

"Hugh," she whispers hard.

He closes his eyes.

"Good night, Hugh," she says.

"Good night," he whispers. "Now go inside. And don't come out again."

"Some freaking vacation," she says, walking away.

When he told her how they'd be spending his time off, she didn't speak to him for three days. He gathered spikes along the railroad tracks, rummaged through the shed for the cinder blocks and wooden crates, bought lumber and nylon cord. He's been stationed outside almost two weeks now, but inside, during the day, he hears the worry in Roberta's voice, her whispers on the phone, and he knows he's losing her. Why has she given up so easily? And why is it so remarkable that he should want to fight back?

Headlights flicker through the trees down Division. He hears an engine's four-cylinder whine, probably Japanese. The vehicle turns onto Rushton, then the engine winds back up, the throb of the stereo almost deafening as the car flies by beneath him, followed by an enormous cloud of dust. Hugh lights another cigarette. At that speed, the mailbox would have been a blur. He'll make it up to Roberta somehow later. Over in the field, bats dip and circle in the moonlight, picking mosquitoes out of the air.

A distant rumble enters his dream, gently pulling him to consciousness, then jerking him awake, the adrenaline putting his body to motion before he's fully aware of what's happening. Crouched in position at the front of the platform, Hugh's hands go over the equipment: spikes, knife, gun, nylon cord.

It's happening.

Down on the other side of Stokley's, maybe halfway toward Whitmore creeps the predator, muffler shot and one cockeyed headlight illuminating the tree tops that line the field across the road. Oh, yes, and it is a wagon, too, a Country Squire with wood paneling most probably, rumbling near the Stokley place and ever so slowly heading for Hugh.

He has the sensation that he's drowning, his lungs shrinking.

It's going to happen.

He closes his eyes to regulate his breathing, and when he opens them, the headlights are out. He takes the gun from the Crown Royal bag and places it on the far side of a spike crate. The wagon's crawling, limping along, the engine through the shot muffler an ominous growl. He unsheathes the knife and holds it against the nylon cord.

Moonlight silhouettes two heads in the front seat. The passenger tips a bottle.

Come on, baby, Hugh thinks. Come on now.

And here they come. Nosing over his property line, inching past his driveway, under the first far branches of the maple.

Brake lights flash red behind the wagon as the front end inches into the kill zone. Faces take shape in the green glow of the dashboard light. Yes, two of them, maybe seventeen, both wearing baseball caps and white tee shirts. The passenger drinks. The driver says something Hugh can't make out over the engine, then they laugh their murderous laughs, throwing back their vandalous heads.

The windshield enters the first kill zone. Hugh's hand shakes as he takes up a railroad spike. It is happening.

He can hear the sounds of their voices but not what they say. The bumper glides by beneath him and then the hood. Cigarette boxes and coffee cups litter the dash. The brake lights flash. The passenger pushes himself out his window, perches on the door with a baseball bat, and Hugh slices into the nylon cord.

There is a moment after the cord snaps and before the crash, the moment when the cinder blocks are falling, that Hugh experiences a sort of ecstatic agony, half wishing to stop what he's started, but hungry for the beautiful crashing sounds of his revenge.

Time changes after that, after it starts to happen. Sounds accumulate. Glass and metal. The back block bounces off the roof of the wagon, but the middle one crashes right through the windshield, followed by the dull thud of the front block landing on the hood, where it seems to be firmly lodged. Hugh upends a crate of spikes, and then the car is moving, fishtailing in the dirt. Screams come from inside, but Hugh doesn't register words, just the sounds of startled fear as the wagon drunkenly weaves away from him, the tires spinning up a roostertail of dust and gravel.

His hands shake violently as he wipes his mouth.

The car weaves out of control, the passenger flopping with the motion before pulling himself half back inside, and then, as the back end of the wagon swerves, the tires gain traction, pushing the speeding car toward the line of trees before McCurdy's place.

The accelerator must be all the way down, the throttle wide open.

"Hey," Hugh calls, but it's like yelling into a storm.

The front end slams into the first tree in line.

Hugh expects the car to bounce, to explode, but it doesn't.

The engine sputters and dies.

Immediately, the sound of crickets and frogs in the back swamp replaces the jarring mechanical roar. But the sound of glass breaking, of metal on metal, and then metal on wood seems to linger.

Hugh throws the rope ladder over the edge and slides to the ground. "Hey!" he calls as he runs toward them. No smoke or steam comes from the front end and nobody seems to be moving. McCurdy's porch light flashes on.

"Hey!" Hugh calls, still running.

The stink of gasoline and exhaust hangs in the air. Hugh notices he's holding a railroad spike and hurls it into the field before reaching the car, which does not have wood paneling. He tastes copper and sand in his mouth, seems to be sucking a mouthful of old pennies. The front seat is a mess, far too crowded with odd, unidentifiable shapes. Glass sparkles in the moonlight over everything. Hugh rips open the door and tries to pull the slumped driver from the car, but he's pinned by the steering wheel, which seems far too close to the seatback. "Come on," Hugh whispers. "Wake up."

He lifts the kid's head, brushes his face, and glass comes off on his hands. *Oh, Jesus*, the kid's face is a mess, *Oh, fuck*, a delicate network of cuts and blotchy bruises already surfacing. The cinder block sits where the armrest should be, but where is the other kid, the passenger? Somebody's missing, maybe dead or waiting to kill him, to outsmart him again, like maybe the whole thing is a set-up.

Hugh tries to arrange the driver so his head will remain erect, but it flops, the chin resting on the bent steering wheel. "Come on," Hugh says, shaking the kid's shoulder in an effort to dislodge him. But the kid won't obey, and then a dark line of blood pushes at the edge of his lips, darker than the other blood on his face, and drips into his lap. Hugh snakes out of his T-shirt and mops at the kid's face, tilting him back by his forehead, but there's so much glass he only seems to cut him up worse, pushing the slivers deeper into all that soft flesh, and the other kid out in the field somewhere bleeding to death.

"Good God," McCurdy says behind him and Hugh jumps, hitting his head on the door frame.

"Call *nine-one-one*," Hugh says. You can practically see the face ballooning up purple under all that blood in the glow of the dashboard light. Hugh drops the chin against the steering wheel. "There might be another one."

McCurdy stands near the open door, shifting his weight from side to side, his pallid face ghostly in the moonlight. "They're on their way."

Hugh runs past him, around the crumpled front end of the car, and stumbles into the field, every bump and furrow, every clump of grass tricking him into thinking he's found it.

Roberta's voice calling his name seems to be part of a dream.

He looks up and sees flashes of light, her fluorescent bathrobe defining her progress as she runs toward the wreck. "Hugh!" she calls, "Are you all right?"

"Turn around!" he screams, frozen in the field. "Go back!"

"Hugh!" she calls, the white robe moving faster.

McCurdy backs out of the car to greet her. Hugh stands motionless. He's got to find the body. He's got to shut her up.

"I think this one's dead," McCurdy says as Roberta reaches the car.

"No he's not!" she says.

She stands at the open driver's door with McCurdy, looking in, then looks toward the field. "What have you done, Hugh?"

"There's been an accident," Hugh says walking toward them through waist high grass. "Don't look, Roberta." And then he steps on him. This is not mud or loose dirt. His foot slides over slimy slickness and then Hugh's on top of him, repulsed and terrified.

"I've found another one!" he yells as he wriggles away from the body. On his knees, frantic, he can see the shiny blackness of the boy's bloody T-shirt, as if it has been dipped in oil, but he can't find the head. Is he losing his mind? Is he delirious? He tries to rearrange the body, to put it in order, to align it properly, but it's not coming together.

"Come here, come here!" he screams, but when he looks up they're already there.

"What is it?" McCurdy says. "I can't see him."

Roberta steps over the body, then kneels beside Hugh, grabbing his wrists and squeezing hard, pulling his hands away from the boy. "Leave him alone," she says. "I told you ... Just leave him alone!"

Sirens sound down Whitmore Road.

Hugh squints at the body hoping to bring the boy's face out of shadows. His hands won't behave. He's trying to get to the shoulders, to feel for the neck, but he can't move his hands or arms. He looks to see Roberta pulling him by the wrists. He tries to crouch, but then he's falling again, right on top of Roberta this time. She pushes him as he scrambles off her.

"Get away!" she yells as she slaps at his chest. Her robe is smeared with black blood.

McCurdy crouches on the other side of the boy. "Jesus God," he says.

The sirens seem to be audible again, seem to be piercingly loud, in fact, though they must not have ever gone away.

Roberta is crying on the ground. "Look what you've done Hugh."

Hugh stands off to the side, watching McCurdy arrange the body now. "I have no idea what you're talking about."

"Hugh, Jesus."

For the first time he becomes aware of the stickiness on his bare chest, on his hands and arms, the warmth of it, on his face, his neck, everywhere. He wipes at his bloody chest with his bloody hands, swirls the white of his skin up through the blood as if he were finger painting.

Doors slam. Men run toward them. McCurdy mumbles something as he stands from the body. Roberta has rolled into a ball.

"See to the boy in the car," McCurdy shouts as he walks toward the men. "This one's dead."

"He is not!" Roberta screeches.

All this blood.

"Get away now," one of the men says. "Don't touch anything."

Still warm, but drying.

The men drop their tool chests and fall to the ground.

Like concrete setting.

Hugh touches Roberta's shoulders, crouches down to help her up. Sirens come from all directions, up Division, down Whitmore. With this much confusion, with the mess in the car, the blood and glass, the coffee cups and empty cigarette packs, it seems possible that the cinder block and spikes will be overlooked, that the empty beer bottles will account for everything.

"Come on, Roberta," Hugh whispers.

She allows herself to be helped up. He leads her toward the road, whispering nonsense in her ear as she leans against his bloody torso.

A police car turns the corner at Division, its blue lights mixing with the red from the ambulance, and the siren screaming all the way to the front of McCurdy's house, where it goes silent. The sheriff gets out.

Hugh guides Roberta through the field and enters the road behind the accident.

Another police car rounds the corner at Whitmore, siren blaring, lights flashing, headlights blinding Hugh as he leads his sleepwalking wife home to bed. The car brakes hard near the maple, then rolls alongside them. The siren goes dead. "Where are you folks going?" a young deputy asks. "Hadn't you ought to get to the hospital?"

Hugh shakes his head, looks at his bloody chest, at Roberta's bloody bathrobe. "It wasn't us," he says. "We tried to help."

Roberta grunts.

He pulls her closer, squeezing her shoulder.

"You sure you're okay?"

Hugh nods toward the accident. "It's back there."

The deputy pulls away.

Roberta twists out of his hold. "Let me go," she growls, and she runs toward the house, away from him.

He climbs the rope ladder to the platform and buries the knife in a crate of spikes with his gun. The lights throb red and blue urgency, and he can hear the static of radios, but he knows the cops can't see or hear him, that they've never cared about him anyway except as a victim. He piles one spike crate on top of the other, then crawls around them to the ladder, *as a victim*, heaving both crates over the edge and descending.

Outside the bathroom window he hears the shower running as he walks around the side of the house. *A victim*. He hides the crates in the dark shed, cluttered with the old tools and junk that were there when he bought the place, then trips over a rusty cultivator, cutting his hand as he falls against it.

Will this lead to some kind of blood poisoning?

He loses track of his worry, is stunned for a moment trying to recall the source of this anxiety, then remembers the bodies.

He gathers his lunch and thermos from the platform. Down the road, the back doors of the ambulance hang open, white light illuminating a gurney with a body strapped to it, no way of telling which one. In the field, perhaps they're searching for the head. If it's even missing. Maybe Hugh can join them, find the head and plant it on a stake in his front yard. Boil the meat from the skull and eat it. The bloody belt of Roberta's bathrobe sticks over the edge of the garbage can on the patio. Hugh removes the lid and shoves the whole mess down deeper, then opens the screen door and walks inside.

The shower is still running. He walks into the fluorescent light of the bathroom and smears the steamed up mirror. He looks like a warrior, painted for battle. He shakes his head at his reflection, trying to recognize himself as the mirror steams back up.

"Hugh?" Roberta says from the shower. "Hugh, is that you?"

He sits on the toilet and takes off his boots and socks, slides his pants down.

"Hugh?"

He pulls the shower curtain aside and steps into the back of the tub.

"Don't touch me, Hugh." She shrinks away from him. "I'm rinsing."

The blood is caked on his chest, but the steam makes it slick again and the fresh blood from the fresh cut runs red instead of the almost black of the dried stuff. Roberta won't look at him. She steps out the front of the tub, and Hugh steps into the hot water, turning it pink as it runs off him.

The sirens start again, over the sounds of the shower, the sounds of her voice.

"Hugh," she says. "For God's sake. Do you hear me?"

The water burns his skin, his scalp. "I'm right here," he says. Or thinks he says.

"Leaving," he hears. Inside? Outside? He can't tell.

He turns up the heat. There are bodies outside, victims. The cops won't see what monsters they were before, what Hugh has really done. How he's saved them, turned them into poor dead boys.

"Hugh," Roberta says, "Listen to me. I said I'm—"

He rips open the shower curtain. Water sprays the bathroom. Roberta's hands fly to her face as he reaches for her.

He would never hurt her. Doesn't she understand anything?

Her towel falls from her body.

"No," she cries. "Hugh!"

He steps out of the tub and lifts her against him.

"I said no!" she cries.

He holds her tighter.

She won't stop thrashing.

It's just the two of them now. Like at the beginning.

He carries her into the tub, thrashing against him, into the burning water. He carries her inside where it's safe.

Dirty Boots

The night Nikki gets caught fucking Sean in the dorm in Durham—Doug the director pounding on the door and saying her name, demanding that she open up this instant—Nikki decides that the program's promise of a happy future isn't worth the constant monitoring, the idiotic puritanism. That the program's promise is worth precisely nothing. She'll never become who they want her to be, or worse, she thinks, she'll become one of them, half dead and full of fear. Sean practically cowers as he pulls his shirt over his head, scrambling around her bed looking for his boxers and shorts. "Nikki," he hisses, "come on. Get up. Do something." But she doesn't want to do anything, not even fuck him anymore.

"Nikki," Doug calls from the hallway. "This is a serious violation. Open the door." He rattles the knob. "Or I will."

She's not going to talk to Doug anymore—Granola Doug, she calls him—not going to answer his questions or beg his forgiveness. But poor Sean is about to cry, may even be crying. "Go out the window," Nikki says, and Doug, slapping the door, says, "I can't hear you, Nikki," and Sean says, "How am I supposed to do that?"

"Hang by your fingertips," Nikki says. "Then drop."

"And break my neck?" Sean says.

"Right now," Doug says, and Sean says, "Get up, Nikki. Come on. Get dressed."

Nikki's not going to get dressed. If they insist on barging into her room uninvited with a pass key, they can face her naked.

"Five seconds," Doug says. "I'm counting down."

"Please," Sean says.

"Five," Doug says.

Sean sits on Karen's bed across the narrow room, still watching Nikki, but not pleading with his eyes anymore, apparently resigned to his punishment, which he must view as catastrophic: expulsion from the program, meaning no more monthly counseling sessions at his high school during the year, but no more summer program at the university either, and worse, no more help clawing his way to college, the only reason any of them are here, the promise of escape, which Nikki now sees as bait for another, bigger trap, creating hope to kill it.

"Four," Doug says.

Most of them won't finish the program at all. Only eight students remain in this year's bridge class, the seniors enrolled in college for fall, while all the ones who've fallen away, who've come and gone the last four years, are already working versions of the shit jobs they'll have the rest of their lives. She's been stupid to believe she could make it through this and go off to college in two years, stupid to believe she could change the future.

"Three," Doug says.

Stupid to believe anything. She can't wait two years to get away from Manchester, two years of her mother watching TV in a man's sleeveless T-shirt or dressed up and out all night, not working though she could—pretending Nikki can save them both, saying last weekend, "I know you're smart enough, Nikki, if you can keep from fucking up. Then maybe we can get out of this shithole and I can start getting better," spending all her nights drunk, all her days dying, poisoned by whatever lingers of the cancer that didn't kill her, or the treatment, or maybe just an idea she can't get over five years after the sickness Nikki had hoped so hard would spare her. But Nikki was just a child then, capable of believing anything: that people could get better, for instance, once they went bad, the reason Upward Bound can't change her—because she's already been changed.

"Two," Doug says. "You better get moving."

Nikki looks at Sean, holding his face in his hands and staring at his shoes. Why would he want to be part of something that promises a future and then yanks it away for fucking? It doesn't make sense that two people rubbing against each other could ruin a chance for college hundreds of days away. But there Sean sits, mourning his lost future, unaware he's been Granola Doug's hostage the last three years, believing he's lost his chance when he never had one. It's not just that his mother's poor and nobody in his family has been to college. The offer of help, or his blind embrace of the offer, is what's really destroyed him.

"One," Doug says.

Sean doesn't know that, though. Might never know it. He believes in magic. Is willing to be saved. And maybe his belief in transformation, escaping who he was born to become, will make it true. Just by believing.

Nikki watches his head jerk to the sound of the key in the lock. Poor Sean. And she's got nothing against him. Except his weakness, which isn't really his fault. "Wait," she calls to Doug. "I'm getting dressed."

"No," Doug says, turning the knob, and Nikki screams, "I am!" And the knob turns back and Doug says, "You have sixty seconds," and Nikki looks at Sean still watching the doorknob, his life draining out of him onto the tile floor.

Two weeks ago—two days ago? two hours ago?—she would have felt the same terror, at least a flicker of the doom Sean now feels, the promised future turning to ashes. She was stupid to let herself be sold on their dream, stupid to forget that hope is what kills you. When she got caught smoking the first week of this summer's session—and that seems so long ago, though it was only last month—Nikki sat in Granola Doug's office, looking at photographs of diseased lungs, her pack of cigarettes on Doug's desk, and she promised—because they were always making you promise here, to love yourself, to believe in yourself, to be the difference, to make every situation positive—she promised as she broke the cigarettes, one by one into Doug's trash can, that she would not smoke again, at least not here on Upward Bound's time. And she kept that promise for several weeks, until she made a new promise, this one to herself, when she bought a pack of cigarettes in Manchester, home for the weekend, her mother gone God knew where, that she would never be caught again, a promise she has now broken.

"Come on," Sean says, standing and offering his hand. "Get dressed now."

The only reason they did it here after hours instead of someplace outside earlier was because it was raining all day and they were so close to the end of their time together, and Karen, Nikki's poor, fat roommate, was home with her prodigal father in Somersworth. And mainly because they wanted to. Because they felt like it. She has no idea how they got caught, if someone heard them or spotted Sean on the wrong floor twenty minutes ago. People get caught and punished here all the time, so it hardly matters how or why.

"Forty seconds," Doug calls.

She takes Sean's hand and pulls him down to the bed.

"Nikki," he says, and she says, "Let's make them wait."

"My mom's gonna kill me."

"Let's block the door."

"With what?" Sean says. He pulls himself from her bed and stands on Karen's side of the room, looking at Nikki, looking at the door, looking at Karen's bed, which, like the dressers and desks, is attached to the floor, everything here attached to the floor so the Upward Bounders can't walk away with anything. They only have their bodies to keep the fuckers out with, plus two chairs, some clothes and books, and Nikki's duffel bag. But she knows Doug won't force the door if they push themselves against it, that he won't risk hurting his precious charity cases or his image of himself as savior.

"Thirty seconds," Doug says.

Nikki stands from her bed, watching Sean watch her body, the body she's made available to him these last few weeks, pretending their first time she was a virgin because he was and it was important to him. And they've fucked and kissed and held each other every chance they've gotten, which hasn't been so often, not often enough, Sean believing, she knows, they're at the beginning of something, Nikki wondering if they're at the end, another reason for taking the chance tonight, because Sean lives all the way up in Berlin at the top of the state, hours and hours and worlds from Manchester, and because he still believes in a safe kind of escape, an entrance into the white shoe world, where he must believe they're saving a space for him, but that's what she likes about him, too, how he still believes, and Doug says, "Twenty seconds," and Nikki shouts, "Will you just give me a fucking minute here, Doug! I can't find my fucking panties, okay?"

"I am giving you a minute," Doug says.

She looks at Sean who looks away. He just needs to be convinced.

"Now fifteen seconds."

She knows there are staff members in the hall with Doug, plus all the students on her floor, getting off on this little drama. There are only two here she'll miss, three counting Sean: Barbara, the residential supervisor, who took her to her own house in Portsmouth two weekends ago when Nikki's mom was in jail, and Jasmine, this wicked funny chick from Dover, a junior like Sean who Nikki got baked with a couple times. They laughed and laughed, wandering the campus, the little town, pretending they were part of it. And even though he's too young, will never be as old as Nikki, and weak, she still feels tenderness for Sean, who just needs to be led.

"Is Barbara out there?" Nikki calls, and after a second in which Nikki imagines Barbara looking at Doug for silent approval to speak, Barbara says, "I'm here, Nikki."

"Can't we just have five minutes so I can get dressed?" she says. "Can't I just have that tiny dignity," dignity being their favorite word, along with trust and commitment and community, words thrown around so carelessly they mean less than nothing.

She hears murmuring on the other side of the door, then Barbra says, "Two minutes, Nikki."

"And not one second more," Doug says.

She looks into Sean's eyes, which won't stay fixed on hers. Why not him? Why not now? If he's so desperate to be saved, why shouldn't she save him? They can save each other. They'll hitchhike somewhere, get jobs. "Let's go," she says, leading him to the window. They're only on the third floor, two flights from the ground and a row of bushes against the brick building to break their fall. But down in the grassy courtyard of Harrison Hall, looking up at Nikki's window, stand three tutor counselors, including Susan, the chick who busted her for smoking.

"One minute," Doug says.

Nikki waves to the crowd below, pulls Sean back from the window. "Wait," she says, "I know how," and Sean says, "You gotta get dressed."

"He'll take us down to the conference room to talk," Nikki says. "But no way he's calling our mothers tonight. Look what happened to Casey. Or Sarah. Not even Jenn got sent home in the middle of the night."

Sean pulls away from her, picks up her tank top from the floor, her skirt, and pushes them toward her.

"We'll wait 'til three o'clock, when everyone's asleep," she says. "Then meet in front of T-Hall and take off."

"And go where?"

"Anywhere."

Barbara told Nikki she was self-destructive, another one of their words here, but taking off seems the opposite of that. Isn't it more self-destructive to be all alone, stuck in Manchester with her living-dead mother?

"Take these," Sean says, the drowning back in his eyes as he pushes her clothes against her. "Please."

"Thirty seconds," Doug says.

Nikki grabs her tank top, pulls it over her head. The worst part will be in the conference room downstairs, watching Sean beg for another chance for next year, shrinking, promising—what, to never fuck again? the moment Nikki will erase him from her memory for good, and if that means eliminating a piece of herself, it's only a tiny piece she won't miss. There's nobody in this world she can talk to. Her cousin Melanie gone to Texas. Crystal still in Manchester, already stuck there forever. Maybe Nikki should beg like Sean, hold her breath for two years, as if anyone could, then go to college with the people they've been training her to join, the people they've been training her not to offend, the fuckers with ruby slippers who were born into it.

She pulls her skirt from Sean's hand, steps into it, closing the hooks and eyes on her hip.

She'd rather be dead.

"Fifteen seconds," Doug says.

She takes Sean's face in her hands, kisses him hard.

"I would," Sean whispers. "If I could. You know I would. It just doesn't make sense. I can take the bus down to Manchester whenever we want."

"I know," Nikki says. "That's exactly what we'll do." She leads him to the door.

They'll ship her back tomorrow, one day early, if they can get hold of her mom, which they won't. More likely she'll wait here with the others, go back to Manchester Friday when she's supposed to go, Sean gone tomorrow, Sean gone tonight, Sean gone in fifteen minutes, half an hour, fifteen seconds, whenever his begging becomes unbearable.

She hears the key slide into the lock. Doug says, "I'm coming in." The doorknob turns, the door cracks open. Nikki throws herself against it as hard as she can, slamming the fuckers back, taking deep breaths as she plants her feet and leans against the wood, planted and pushing, Doug howling in the hall, Sean behind her doing nothing to save them, until he wraps Nikki in his arms and pulls her back, lifting her from the floor, her legs kicking. Doug crashes through the door, his hand pressed over his bleeding nose, his red face furious. "I didn't do it," Sean says holding Nikki in the air. And she thrashes and thrashes, clawing and kicking his horrible words, blood running over Doug's mouth and chin, dripping, as he reaches for her, Sean yelling, "She didn't mean it."

"I did mean it," Nikki snarls, "you goddamn fucker," and she thrashes and thrashes, clawing and kicking, Doug and Sean grunting as she thrashes and kicks.

Germans

Henry could have shot all three of them from where he sat, wedged into the crotch of a maple, but he knew they wouldn't die. "You missed," they'd say, and then they'd kill him. If they weren't liars, they would admit there was no hiding from the Gestapo—secret rooms, new identities, none of it worked—but they were liars. Henry made his hands into binocular tubes and watched the Allies reach Danny's lawn, where they dropped their guns and went inside. Henry counted to a hundred before lowering himself from the tree. The coast was clear, but he counted off another fifty, then zigzagged across the field in a crouch, zigzagged across the lawn, grabbing weapons, and he kept running until he reached his temporary headquarters.

Inside, Charlotte was screaming her head off.

His mother walked the baby from room to room.

Henry took two oatmeal health cookies from the cookie jar.

His mom said, "Hi, honey," over the screaming baby. Henry said hi back and made his way upstairs. If a kidnapper broke into the house late at night when his father was away on business, Henry would take the pocketknife from his dad's top dresser drawer and kill the intruder. They didn't know he knew about the knife, but he did.

There were a lot of things they didn't know.

Like about Mr. Boerman's pirate walk, how he swung his wooden leg straight from the hip. And on the second day of school, it was Henry he noticed staring at his jerky mechanical walk. "You want to know about my leg, is it?" he said. "Why I walk like this?"

Henry knew why Mr. Boerman walked like that.

The other kids looked at their desks, sneaking peeks at Henry as his face went hot.

"A handicap's nothing to be ashamed of," Mr. Boerman said. "And I understand your curiosity." He walked in front of the class between his desk and the blackboard, showing off his wooden leg, looking right at Henry as he explained his injury: a story about a milk truck running him over during the depression. Hospitals and rehabilitation and speckles of spit flying, the stiff leg swinging and sweat running down his sideburns just as it had when the Gestapo held him for questioning—before they took a hacksaw to his thigh to get the necessary information. Behind his thick glasses, Mr. Boerman probably had a fake eye that he took out at night, covering the pink oozing hole with a leather patch.

At dinner, Henry told his father he'd been in a fight at school.

"A fight?" his mother said, wiping carrot paste from Charlotte's chin. "Henry, what are you talking about?"

His dad pushed a forkful of waxed bean mashed potato hamburger casserole into his mouth.

"A kid pushed me," Henry said. "At the jungle gym." It could have happened.

Charlotte knocked her sippy cup from her highchair tray. His mother picked it up and said, "Henry, we don't approve of fighting."

"Danny started it," Henry said.

"I won't have fighting," his mom said.

The baby threw her sippy cup over Henry's shoulder. His dad took another big bite while Henry's mom pulled the baby from her highchair and talked baby talk. "It can be tough being new," his dad said. "Can't it?"

"Rick," his mom said, "don't encourage."

"No fighting," she said on her way out of the kitchen. "And I mean it."

Henry didn't tell his dad about being the Germans or what really happened on the playground, which was nothing, except that Ronny Hanson sat next to him on the merry-go-round and started talking.

Henry saw Eric and Paul Stone running around the jungle gym. He saw Paul Stone see him with Ronny, who was saying something about his meteorology kit. When Ronny put his hand on Henry's shoulder, and said, "Wanna come over after school?" Henry slapped his hand away and shouted, "You're the Viet Cong!"

"Did you push him back?" his father asked.

Henry nodded.

"You know we don't approve of fighting," his father said. He scooped a forkful of vomit casserole from Henry's plate. "Go watch some TV," he said. "We'll have ice cream when your mother comes down."

For a long time after his brother died inside his mother, back in New Jersey, before Baltimore and now Michigan, Henry thought his unknown brother was only missing. His mom had often talked about the new baby. She'd put Henry's hand over the dome of her belly and Henry could feel it moving around—kicking, his mom said. But when she went to the hospital, the baby came out dead. And even though they'd explained to Henry that the baby was dead, his mom always referred to it as lost. She had lost the baby, she'd tell people. Even later, in Baltimore, and now Michigan, she might say to someone, "I lost my second. Charlotte's really my third."

Now that he was almost nine Henry knew that the baby was dead, but he still thought of him wandering around New Jersey, lost. Maybe under the big beer bottle in Newark, as tall as a smokestack, that they passed on their way to his grandmother's house in Connecticut. And each move seemed to make it less likely that the baby would ever be found. Like if he'd somehow made it to Baltimore, crawling along the beltway, there was no way he'd find them here.

After they moved to Michigan, Henry got bunk beds and a desk. He'd always wanted bunk beds, but he wondered if his parents wanted them too, to have an open bed if his brother ever did show up.

Ronny had slept in the top bunk the night he stayed over a few weeks after Henry moved in. He lived at the bottom of the hill and rode by on his old-fashioned bike the day the moving truck arrived. Ronny's mom, Mrs. Hanson, had a purple mark over the left side of her face. Henry and Ronny rode bikes that first day, but when Ronny wanted to show off his meteorology kit, Mrs. Hanson gave them Rice Krispie treats, which Henry was afraid to eat because of that thing on her face.

Everybody else was at camp then—Paul Stone, Eric, Danny—but Ronny couldn't go to camp because of asthma. Ronny had a stamp collection. Ronny had a Lionel train. Ronny showed him a dead deer in the woods behind his house. Then the other kids came back from camp and Henry had to be a German with Ronny every time they played war.

Danny's mom bought Twinkies and let you watch *Dark Shadows*. Eric's brother was in Vietnam. Paul Stone's dad was a policeman and kept pictures of naked ladies, which Paul Stone sometimes snuck out of the house. Henry's dad designed weapons systems and had killed people in World War Two, which, the two times Henry mentioned it, none of the other kids believed. When Ronny slept over and didn't believe him, Henry called his dad to his room, but his dad said it wasn't something to talk about. Then, just yesterday, when Eric was bragging about his brother in Vietnam greasing gooks and Henry said big deal, his dad had killed Nazis, Ronny, who nobody ever listened to, said it was a lie and the other kids believed him. Before, Henry had felt kind of sorry for Ronny, with his asthma and Keds, always having to be the Germans. Now he hated him.

The next day at school, Henry got in trouble for drawing a swastika. If he'd known it was such a big deal he wouldn't have put one at the bottom of his spelling quiz. The funny part was he didn't know he'd done it. There was a lot of stuff at the bottom of his page—a house, a seagull, a tank, a guy with glasses and a stove pipe hat, and the swastika. At the end of reading, right before the recess bell rang, Mr. Boerman said, "Henry, stay back from recess, please," and, of course Henry knew he'd done something wrong and then the bell rang and he was alone with Peg Leg.

"Henry," Mr. Boerman said, standing from his desk and swivel-walking down Henry's row, "just so you know: my ancestry's Dutch, not German."

Henry had no idea what the old man was talking about.

"This might not mean much to you," Mr. Boerman said, "but I lost two brothers in the war—one in Italy and one in France."

"My dad was in the Battle of the Bulge," Henry said.

Mr. Boerman placed the spelling quiz on Henry's desk and stood over him. "Then I would think you'd know better," he said.

Henry looked at the piece of paper. All the answers were right, but at the bottom with his other drawings was the swastika, circled and underlined in red ink.

Henry looked at Mr. Boerman looking down at him. He looked at the swastika. It looked funny, backwards or upside down. "Did I make it wrong?" he said.

Mr. Boerman snatched up the quiz and jerked back toward his desk. "Put your head down," he said.

Henry put his head down. He had never been in trouble at school.

"I'm writing a note to your father," Mr. Boerman said, "and I expect a reply."

Henry smelled his desk against his face and listened to kids outside screaming. If the Red Chinese came creeping out of the woods with machine guns, he and Mr. Boerman would probably be the only survivors, hidden in a secret room under the basement. Or maybe Mr. Boerman wouldn't make it because of his leg. Maybe the Red Chinese would assassinate Mr. Boerman at his desk as he wrote the letter to Henry's father.

The baby was down for a nap when Henry got home. His mom put a plate of oatmeal health cookies and some apple juice on the kitchen table. The letter was folded in his back pocket. On the bus ride home Paul Stone had taken Ronny's glasses and wouldn't give them back until Ronny cried and then Shirley the bus driver had to pull over and Paul Stone got written up. They'd both gotten in trouble that day. But at the bus stop, before Henry could comment on that, Paul Stone said, "I want my rifle back, Tyler."

Henry started to walk. "I didn't take it," he said.

"Yeah you did," Paul Stone said. His house was in the other direction, but he was following Henry.

"Me too," Eric said.

"I mean it, Tyler," Paul Stone said, and then they walked the other way. When they were pretty far back and Henry was almost home, he shouted, "I didn't take your stupid guns!" but he couldn't tell if they'd heard him. They were around the corner already.

"What did you do in school today?" his mom asked. She stood at the counter making bread, rolling dough on his dad's old drafting board. She always asked that question. Henry asked for another cookie.

His mom put two cookies on a plate with horses on it.

"Did you have a good day?" she said, turning back to her bread.

The Polish had horses in the war that got slaughtered in the blitzkrieg. They were stupid to think they could beat tanks with horses. "I got in trouble," Henry said. He pulled the envelope from his pocket. "Mr. Boerman wrote a letter."

His mother turned to face him, but her hands kept working the dough. "What do you mean you got in trouble?"

"I have to bring a letter back."

"Henry," his mother said, wiping her hands on a dish cloth and walking to the table. "What did you do?"

"I drew a picture," he said. "I don't know what I did," he said.

He handed her the letter. "It's for Dad," he said.

He watched her open the envelope and read Mr. Boerman's words. She squinted at Henry, squinted at the letter. He couldn't tell what she thought.

"Go ahead and get changed," she finally said, putting the letter back in its envelope. "We'll talk about this later."

Upstairs, he walked into Charlotte's room and looked at her sleeping in her crib. He wished she could talk already. She didn't know about their brother yet. Maybe the note was no big deal. Maybe he could blame Ronny for the guns. Charlotte stretched in her sleep, rolled over. "We have a brother," Henry whispered in her ear, "who lives in a secret beach house, in Cape May, New Jersey." The baby didn't move. Henry walked to his room and waited to be called down.

At the dinner table, his father's bottom lip stuck out as he read the note and looked at the spelling quiz. Charlotte sat in her highchair across from Henry. His mother pulled potatoes from the oven. His father put the spelling test in front of Henry and pointed at the swastika. "You know what this is, right?"

Henry nodded.

His mother put plates on the table. "It's a horrible symbol," she said.

"That's right," his father said. He pointed to the picture of the man with glasses and a stove pipe hat. "Who's this?" he said.

It wasn't anybody. Henry remained silent.

"Okay," his father said. He picked up the papers and folded them. Henry's mom started feeding Charlotte. His dad cut at his Swiss steak. "You remember when your mom didn't like to look at babies," he said, "or got sad when she saw babies?"

Henry remembered his mother crying in the grocery store.

"That was because it reminded her of losing Tommy."

His mother fed peas to the baby on a tiny spoon.

"The swastika—"

"Which is an ugly symbol," his mother said.

"Which is an ugly symbol," his father said, "reminds Mr. Boerman of the brothers he lost in the war. And how he didn't go, maybe." He jammed a big bite of Swiss steak into his mouth and chewed.

"He's sensitive about it," his mother said. "But Rick, tell him how ugly it is."

His father swallowed. "These Nazis," he said, "did horrible things to people. Things you can hardly believe."

"I know," Henry said. Didn't his dad remember how often they watched *The World at War?*

"You don't know," his father said. "You can't imagine."

His mother said, "These people were evil."

"They gassed people in showers," Henry said, "burned them in ovens. They hunted people down and killed them."

"That's right," his father said, sawing his meat.

Henry's mother put her hand on top of Henry's hand and leaned over her plate, looking at him hard. "And when you make that symbol," she said, "people might think—"

Charlotte shrieked and Henry's mother loaded another spoonful of peas.

"It's not a cool symbol," his father said.

"Eat your dinner, honey," his mother said.

Henry picked up his knife and fork. They didn't know anything. It was a cool symbol. A scary, cool symbol. That didn't mean you didn't hate the Nazis or anything.

"It just gives the wrong impression, honey," his mother said. "It's not something you want to even think about."

Henry's face felt hot. The Swiss steak was in a reddish-orange goopy sauce that could have been blood. He didn't do it, but he thought about tracing a swastika in that sauce right on top of his flat leathery steak, imagined each forbidden line he would make so that it was just the same as actually doing it.

"Are we clear on this," his father said. "That it's not a cool symbol?"

Henry choked down a bite of steak. He was going to cry. For no reason he was going to cry and they were going to ask him why he was crying and he'd shake his head and snot would run down his face and he'd cry harder and his dad would think he was a big baby who didn't know anything. He concentrated on his potato and thought about the peasants in Russia, who weren't dirty commies yet but still our friends, eating moldy potatoes before the Nazis killed them with machine guns in a big old potato field. All those dead peasants rotting in a pile. The flies and empty eye holes. But he couldn't stop it. And for a second after it started—this awful crying noise—before his mother jumped from her chair and took him in her arms, they all looked at him, the dirty Nazi, even the baby, confused and horrified by this stranger at their dinner table, crying and gasping for no reason at all.

Something Awful

"Can you light this, Jack?" Sally says, bending with a cigarette in her mouth and handing me a book of matches. "I can't make these things work." The matches are soaked. I don't know if she's looking for trouble or not. Both Joe and Elaine must be watching from the other couch as I hold my lighter to her cigarette and try not to look down her sweater. "Thanks, sweetie," she says over the roar of the Pistons game. As she walks away, Joe and Mark resume their discussion—small caps, large caps, this fund versus that fund, no-load. I don't know what any of it means.

Joe and Sally live down the street from us, Mark and Beth farther away. They're nice enough, but most of the time they'll bore you to tears. We've only been in Michigan six months, and for some reason, they invite us to their barbecues and drinking parties. And for some reason, we attend. Everybody has kids, except us, and this sets us apart and makes us suspect: how lucky we are, yet how unfortunate. Selfish maybe.

Elaine returns to my couch and puts her glass in front of my face, meaning, Make me another drink, so I do.

"Thanks, honey," she says when I hand her the glass.

She passes me a joint.

Sally sits on the couch arm beside me. "What about me?" she says.

I give her the joint.

"What about you?" Joe says, turning off the TV.

She takes a big hit and shrugs. "I don't know," she says.

Joe puts on some awful old music, Genesis or Journey, and Sally starts dancing. She knows her body, seems comfortable with the way it will move. "Come on, Sally," Joe says. He rubs her shoulders. "We'll play a game."

She's wearing a black cotton sweater with little pearl buttons, the top ones undone, and when she throws her arms back, it rides halfway up her stomach so you can see the beginning of her ribs.

"Come on and sit down," Joe tells her.

But Sally keeps dancing, twisting to the music, demonstrating that she's still a viable candidate, even after a baby.

Joe takes her arm and pulls her toward the other couch. "We'll play a game," he says. "Okay, mama?" He places her on the couch and puts on some different awful music, some kind of fusion nightmare, then stands above us rubbing his hands together, and says, "Trivials or Pictionary?"

Mark shrugs. Beth takes her glass into the kitchen. Sally's sweater hikes up her belly again as she slouches into the couch. Between the buttons, I catch glimpses of her bra, black, with a purple flower between the cups. Joe pulls her up, straightening her. "Up we go," he says. She takes it all very well.

"Trivials or Pictionary?" Joe says again.

Elaine digs her fingernails into my palm. She hates these kinds of games, but I don't know what to do. I can't keep my mind off Sally.

Beth returns with a fresh drink.

"What'll it be, Beth?" Joe says, and she says, "You decide."

"Trivials, then," Joe says, and he walks into the back room.

"I like Pictionaries better," Mark says.

"I need a drink," Sally says.

Joe returns with the game and starts setting it up on the enormous glass coffee table.

"Can't we just talk?" Beth says.

"Don't you want to play?" Joe says.

Sally returns with her drink.

"I hate this game," she says, and I say, "Everyone does."

Elaine gives me a look.

Joe seems hurt, sitting on his knees setting up the game. "Well, we don't have to play," he says. "I don't want to force anyone."

Elaine says, "Maybe we could play a different game."

"Maybe Pictionaries," Mark says.

"No," I say. "They're all awful."

Elaine gives me another look. I'm stoned and in trouble, and, for some reason, I don't care.

"We've got to play something," Joe says. He's putting the plastic pieces back in the box.

"What about Something Awful?" I say.

They all look at me.

"He's making this up," Elaine says. "To be cute."

"No," I say, "it's a game I know," wondering when Elaine dropped out of our conspiracy—a month ago, two months ago, tonight?

Sally's eyes are shiny from the booze. "Let's play that," she says.

"How do you play?" Joe asks.

Elaine watches me.

"You tell a story," I say, "something you did—no, the worst thing you ever did. You can cover up certain facts or make them different, but the idea has to be the same."

They're quiet for a second, and then Joe says, "What's the object?"

Sally slaps his shoulder. "All Joe cares about is winning."

"The object is to have done the worst thing," I say. "We'll vote at the end."

Beth says, "That's kind of gross," and Mark squints at me.

"Maybe," I say, "it can be whoever *feels* the worst about what they did."

"See?" Elaine says. "He's making it up."

"But how would we measure that?" Joe says.

"Oh, who cares," Sally says. "Let's just play."

Joe says, "I'd better check on the kids first," and Elaine leans toward me and whispers, "Don't be around people if you're just going to mock them," and I say, "What?" and she shakes her head, pissed, then hands me her glass for another drink.

When I come back from the kitchen, Sally is on the little expensive couch perpendicular to the big expensive couch where Elaine and I sit. Beth and Mark are on the floor across the table from us. Joe turns down the music and joins Sally, then rubs his hands together again. "Who's going to start?" he says.

Mark pulls a joint from his pocket and lights it. Elaine passes it to me without taking a hit.

I'm actively ignoring Elaine when Beth says, "I think I've got one. I mean, it may not be exactly right—"

"Sure it is," I say.

She sits up and smooths her skirt. Everybody watches her, waiting. "I mean, this didn't go on that long. Longer than it should have, I guess, and I never got caught. That's the thing."

"What was it?" Sally says.

Beth takes a long drink, bringing up the tension. "It wasn't much," she says, finally, and Mark says, "Well, what?"

"I stole things," Beth says.

"Shoplifting?" I say.

"It started when I was twelve," she says. "Just gum and little stuff. Combs, barrettes."

Sally and Elaine lean toward her.

"Teenage girls do these things," Beth says, and Elaine says, "Yep," meaning she's back in the room, that I might be forgiven.

"On a dare," Sally says.

"Then it got to be expensive stuff," Beth says, "and it wasn't a group thing anymore. I mean, I didn't tell anybody I was stealing these things."

Joe says, "Like what?" and Beth takes another long drink.

"It became a private thing," she say. "Jewelry, clothes. You know, expensive underwear."

"I did that," Sally says.

"But not for this long," Beth says. "A lot of times I just threw the stuff away and felt kind of guilty and embarrassed."

"How long?" Mark asks her.

"Not that long," she says.

"Did I know you?" he says.

"It stopped in college. I stole a pair of expensive sunglasses. That's not easy. They keep them locked up, and I had to have about twelve pairs on the case and sneak one in my purse when the guy wasn't looking."

"Why was that the last time?" Elaine says. "What made you stop?"

"I don't know," Beth says. "It wasn't—"

"Are we supposed to vote on this?" Joe says.

"Is this awful?" I ask Beth, teaming up with Elaine on the inquisition. "Do you feel awful?"

"Guilty maybe," she says. "It's just that I never got caught."

"Rebellion thing," Sally says. "Not awful."

"It did go on a long time," Joe says.

"A little klepto," Mark says.

"So do we vote on this?" Joe says.

"It's just a wrong thing I did," Beth says.

Joe stands and rubs his hands together. "Who needs a drink?" he says, but no one responds.

"I have to think of one," Mark says.

"I want one," Sally calls to Joe in the kitchen.

I feel let down by Beth's crime. I look at Elaine. She half-smiles. I never used to worry about her approval. I half-smile back.

Mark extends his legs under the coffee table, squinting and scratching his head.

"What about me?" Sally says, when Joe returns with one drink.

"We can share this one, Mama," he says, sitting on the floor at her feet.

"I've got one," Mark says, and everybody looks at him, waiting.

"It was in college," he says. "In the house."

"Your frat house?" Joe says.

"It seemed bad then," Mark says. "But not—" He runs a hand through his hair. "It would probably be a rape today, but not—"

"What?" Beth says.

"That's why frats should be illegal," Elaine says, and both Mark and Joe stare at her.

"Rape?" Sally says, repositioning herself behind Joe.

I look at Sally and she's staring at me, her mouth open a little. Her sweater has pink yarn flowers on it I would like to bite off. She smiles, doesn't disengage eye contact, so I'm relieved when Beth says, "Are you telling me you took part in a rape?"

"I didn't take part," he says, "but, whatever it was—not rape then—whatever it was, I walked in near the end."

"And you didn't do anything?"

Sweat's popping on his forehead.

"I'm not sure what happened exactly."

"I'm gonna be sick," Beth says.

"Fine," Mark says. "I shouldn't have brought it up."

"You finish it now you've started," she tells him.

I look at Sally and she looks right back, smiles again. It sends a shiver through me.

"It was near the end of junior year," Mark says. "Pledge night, everybody's drunk—"

"I can't listen to this," Elaine says, starting to rise.

I take her hand and bring her back down to the couch. "Let him finish."

Beth says, "All right, then, finish."

Elaine digs her fingernails into my palm.

"We'd run out of beer," Mark says, "but there were two reserve kegs for when everybody left. I was looking for a cup."

He takes a drink. "Give me one of those cigarettes," he says to Sally, and she throws him the pack.

"Finish," Beth says.

"I will if you'll let me."

"Go ahead."

"There's this storage room down a long hall in the basement," he says, lighting the cigarette and blowing smoke over our heads.

Beth says, "Will you—" and Mark says, "I am. Just. So, okay. I open the door and she's there on the floor, but, I mean, fucked up, like her eyes rolling back in her head. And somebody, you know, on top of her, and two brothers smoking and watching, making jokes, or whatever, and it's horrible, but she's not screaming or fighting or anything, but, you know, seems to be enjoying it—"

"Right," Elaine says. "Kind of like surgery."

"Who were the brothers?" Joe says.

"Let him finish," Beth says.

"I know it was wrong," Mark says. "The chick doesn't even know I'm there. That's how bad it is. And Rick's the one that's—"

"Rick Altman?" Joe says.

"But I don't do anything, don't say anything—"

"Until you run upstairs and call the police," Sally says.

"I'm like paralyzed," Mark say. "Mitch closes the door and puts his arm around me."

"Mitch O'Connor?" Joe says, and Mark rolls his eyes and says, "It doesn't matter."

"Mitch O'Connor?" Beth says. "I can not believe this."

"So you did her too," Sally says.

Elaine digs her fingernails into my palm. Mark shakes his head widely.

"This is before anybody talked about date rape," he says, and Beth says, "You did it, too?"

"Let me finish," Mark says. "Mitch kept talking with his arm around me. 'She's loving it,' he says, and she's making all the right sounds, like she is loving it. But just by the way he's talking, I know how wrong it is, and there are supplies everywhere on steel shelves, paper towels and silverware and stuff."

"But, finally, you do her, too," Sally says.

I look at her and she's grinning, playing with a piece of her hair, twirling it around her finger, scaring the hell out of me.

Mark says, "I'm sick about it. I'm like, 'I'm just getting these cups,' and I have to step right over her to get to the shelf."

"Oh my God," Beth says.

"But the feel in the room is different, because they see I'm not going to do it. And then I'm gone, out of there, freaking out in shock—"

"What happened to the woman?" Elaine says, and Mark says, "I don't know."

"Did you talk about this?" Beth says. "Did you confront them?"

"I never said a word about it."

"Don't you think that's cowardly?" Elaine says.

"That's what I'm saying," Mark says. "I should have done something."

"You could still do something," Elaine says.

"That was fifteen years ago."

"Yeah," Beth says, "but Mitch still comes by when he's in town."

"And for years," Sally says, "you thought about it and jerked off."

Elaine sighs—or grunts—disgusted, and Joe says, "Hey," turning to face her. "That's not right."

"He's never coming over again," Beth says. "You see to that. We have a child. What about me? You let a rapist in the house?"

"I didn't know what it was exactly."

"Well that's definitely worse than Beth's," Joe says.

"I'm getting a drink," Mark says, and he walks to the kitchen.

Elaine says, "Sick."

"At least he told the whole story," I say.

Sally looks at me, and says, "How do you know?"

"I can not believe this," Beth says.

"What about you, Joe?" Sally says. "Did you rape any drunk chicks at the house?"

Joe shakes his head. "You heard about it, though," he says.

When Mark comes back from the kitchen, he says, "I know it was horrible. I'm not saying it wasn't horrible." He tries to take Beth's hand, but she swats him away.

Elaine hands me her glass.

"Are you sure?" I ask, and she nods, not looking at me.

"Maybe this isn't such a good idea," I say.

"Just make it," Elaine says.

"It's getting late," Mark says, and Sally says, "But we haven't finished."

I walk into the kitchen feeling as if I've taken part in something that should be reported to the authorities. The ice bucket is empty, so I take some trays from the freezer and while I'm twisting them over the sink, I feel her press up against me and grind.

I drop the tray and spin. Sally's there, smiling. I take her by the shoulders and push her back. She keeps smiling as she twists out of my hold and rubs herself against me, cupping my crotch with her right hand.

"Hi there," she says.

"Come on," I say in a strangled whisper, "I can't do this. Someone will come in." I've never cheated on my wife, never wanted to be the kind of guy that cheats on his wife.

"Well, when, then?" she says, and I say, "I don't know. I'm making this drink."

She moves her face toward me, keeps the smile on, like she's amused by my childish antics. When she brushes her face against mine and licks around my ear, she smells like shampoo and cigarettes and perfume and garlic and baby powder, and I can hardly breathe.

"Okay," I say, "all right." I push her away again.

She grabs me one more time and squeezes as she turns to walk out of the kitchen, shaking her ass like a little girl imitating a woman imitating a hooker.

Only Beth and Elaine are in the living room when I return, both silent and staring.

"Where is everybody?" I say, and then Sally and Joe walk in from the back rooms. "Joe tried to rape me in the baby's room," Sally says, laughing, and Joe rolls his eyes.

I try to hide in the couch.

"That's not funny, Sally," Elaine says. "There's nothing funny about rape."

"It was just a joke," Sally says.

"But it's not funny."

"It's okay, Elaine," Beth says, and Elaine says, "I wasn't defending you, Beth. I just don't think it's something to joke about."

I wish she'd let it die.

"And you're right," Joe says.

"Oh, what do you know, Joe," Sally says.

Mark sits at the coffee table and begins rolling a joint. Beth puts her hand on his head, and he turns to her, smiling.

We have to get away from these people.

"Christ," Sally says, "nobody's telling the truth here. I'll give you something awful. How about wanting to kill your baby? How about wishing your husband would die on the way home from work one rainy afternoon?"

"What are you talking about?" Joe says.

We're going to have to get away from everyone.

"Come on," she says. "Willy screamed the first two months he was home. Don't tell me you didn't once, sometime in the middle of the night, just once, so tired, think about letting go and throwing him through the wall."

"Oh my God," Beth says. "I never felt that way about Amy."

"Yeah, sure."

"It got frustrating," Joe says, "but I never felt like that."

"I love my baby," Beth says.

"Sure you do," Sally says. "And you love Mark, too. But that doesn't mean you don't sometimes wish he were dead."

"That's not true."

That is true.

"What are you talking about?" Joe says.

Mark takes a deep hit. Elaine takes a hit, but I pass this time. I'm far too stoned.

"Sally doesn't want you or the baby dead, Joe," Elaine says. "She just thinks of possibilities in her life."

I look at Sally and she smiles. "I do think of possibilities," she says.

"I'm sure you do, Sally," Elaine says.

"When Joe had his affair, for instance, sure, I thought about revenge, my own little fling."

"What?" Joe says, and he laughs, but the red in his face gives him away.

"Oh, come on," Sally says. "We're all friends, here. Right, Mark? Right, Jack?"

"Sure," Mark says. "But—"

"So Joe was fucking this Deadhead chick. I was seven months pregnant. Joe met a little girl from the college. Where was it Joe, a coffee shop?"

"I really don't—"

"Was it because I wasn't putting out?"

I look at Elaine looking hard at Joe. The room needs to be quarantined. But first we have to escape. I try to catch her attention with a head movement, but she won't look.

"Why not bring it all out?" Sally says.

"I think we'd better get going," Beth says, and Sally says, "But we're not done with the game. I'm helping Joe with his Something Awful, here, aren't I, honey?"

She musses his hair.

He jerks away. "This is idiotic," he says. "I have no idea—"

"Oh come on, Joe," Elaine says.

Her voice cuts through me. I grab her hand. "This is none of our business," I say, but she pulls away from me.

Sally leans forward on the little couch close to Joe's face. "Was it wrong of me to hate you for that?"

He's being careful, controlled, but his hands tense like claws.

"Did you honestly think I didn't know? I mean, do I look like an idiot?"

She musses his hair again, but this time he grabs her by the wrist and squeezes, then carefully moves her hand away.

"What was her name?" Sally says. "Sunshine?"

Joe rises to his feet, starts moving around the room. "This is ridiculous," he says. "I have no idea what you're talking about."

"We really have to go," Beth says, standing. "Maybe you guys need some alone time."

Sally sits like Buddha, crosslegged and smiling on the couch.

"Maybe we're all just a little too buzzed," Mark says.

"I didn't do shit," Joe says.

"Well, then," Sally says, "maybe this is my Something Awful."

"That's not funny, Sally," Elaine says.

"Oh, what do you know. I'm just trying to let you liars off the hook. Of course he fucked her. He probably still is."

Joe turns toward the stereo, the back of his neck red. "This is not even true," he says.

I wonder how long my toes have been curled in my shoes. It's just a bad TV show, really. Nothing I'm a part of. Amusing, possibly.

"Please don't leave, Beth," Sally says. "You know how Joe gets."

"What?" Joe says, turning.

"Honey," Elaine says to Sally, "do you want to stay with us tonight?" and I'm thinking, Wait a minute, then saying it: "Wait a minute, here. We're butting in," but Elaine ignores me. "You can stay with us," she says.

I look at Joe, shaking my head, No.

Sally bows her head.

"I'm going to get Amy," Beth says to Mark. "Would you get our coats, honey?"

I take Elaine's hand and squeeze until she looks at me. My teeth are grinding as I make another head movement toward the kitchen. "Can I talk to you in private?" I say, and we rise together, numb, and seem to float into the kitchen, where a rage begins to pour out of me. "Just what are you trying to do here?" I ask her. "We shouldn't have heard any of this. She is not coming over."

"You saw his eyes," she hisses back. "God knows what he's capable of."

"No," I say, our faces close together. "He's a gentle man." As if I know. As if I care.

"Sally told me he's violent."

Behind us one of the babies starts to cry.

I feel like I've been up for ninety-five hours.

"She might be lying," I say. "This might be a game."

Elaine glares at me.

"She seems capable of anything."

"And he doesn't?"

"We hardly even know them."

"I couldn't live with myself if something happened."

"Nothing's going to happen," I say. "I don't want her in my house."

"You could have fooled me," Elaine says.

"What's that supposed to mean?"

I have to be very careful. With my eyes I have to communicate a perfect combination of innocence and indignation.

"Fine," Elaine says "We'll go home. And if something happens, I will never fucking forgive you."

I follow her out of the kitchen.

Beth is changing Amy's diaper on the coffee table, Mark behind her with her coat over his arm. Joe and Sally sit on the love seat. Amy makes gurgling noises and smiles up at us. Joe looks exhausted, but he's holding Sally's hand and caressing it.

"We talked it out," Sally says to me and Elaine. "I told him everything."

Mark stares at the floor, shifting his weight back and forth. Beth wipes the baby's butt.

"He admitted it once I showed him the underwear," which she waves as evidence. "It was wedged in the back seat of the Saab." She holds it out to us, as if we might like to sniff it, but none of us move.

"And I told him about us, Jack," she says, looking at me.

Adrenaline pumps to my fingers and toes, bringing on tremors. I'm as good as guilty, but in a snotty, shaky voice, I say, "What about us, Sally?"

Elaine looks at my profile. Joe looks at Sally's hand in his own. The baby coos.

"Our kissy, rub-rub in the kitchen," Sally says. "Dry humping there by the sink. Making plans."

I laugh incredulously, but it sounds phony even to my ears.

"Okay," Joe says. "It's over."

Elaine cocks her head, sizing me up.

"That's not true," I say.

Beth hands Mark the dirty diaper which he puts in a plastic bag.

"Come on," Mark says to Beth, "we gotta go." They exchange baby and coat. I feel sentenced and forgotten as Joe and Sally rise to bid their friends good-night, handshakes from Joe and kisses from Sally. "We love you guys," Sally says. "Sorry about the scene."

"This is a lie," I say, but no one seems to hear. Elaine takes the baby and kisses her cheek, then hugs Mark and Beth and says good-bye.

Mark shakes my hand. "Maybe at our house next time," he says, and then they're out the door.

Joe helps Elaine with our coats at the hall closet. Sally smiles at me.

"Tell them it's a lie," I say.

Joe hands me my coat. Elaine won't look at me.

"It didn't happen, Joe," I say.

He looks at the floor.

"Thanks a lot you guys," Elaine says. She lets Sally kiss her cheek, but Sally looks at me over her shoulder.

"Tell her it's a lie, Sally," I say, and Elaine says, "Shut up, Jack, it was obvious." She hugs Joe good-bye. Now we start growing old together.

Sally walks forward as if to hug me, but I hold my hands up to keep her away. "Oh, all right," she says. "It's a lie. Feel better?"

"Come on, Jack," Joe says. "Too much to drink."

Elaine's out the door.

Joe turns away.

Sally takes my arm, but I jerk it from her and walk outside.

Elaine stands by the passenger side of the car, waiting for me to unlock her door. I touch her back. She winces.

A crash sounds from inside the house, a vase, an ashtray.

"I didn't do that," I say.

They're screaming at each other. Another crash.

"Yeah, you did," Elaine says. "We'll call the cops when we get home."

I stand outside the open door and bend down to her. "You've got to believe I didn't do that," I say.

She shakes her head rapidly and closes her eyes. "I can't talk to you," she says. "I can't hear you."

I close the door on her and walk to my side of the car, knowing we won't call the cops when we get home. Inside, there's another crash. I open my door and crawl in next to Elaine. She won't acknowledge me. I crank the engine and pull out of the driveway. Elaine looks out her window, as far from me as she can be. "You don't really believe," I say, and Elaine says, "Shut up, Jack. And, please, please spare me the worst things you've ever done. I don't want to know." I drive the three blocks home in silence. The worst things, it seems, are all in front of us.

Heavy Bag

Billy leans his shoulder into the heavy bag, holding it for me as I punch hell out of the bad guy's ribs, the sting spiderwebbing through the thin gloves and out over my knuckles. Billy grunts with each powerful, almighty, mid-section blow I deliver. "Kill him," he says, grunts: "Kill him again." I land one on the outside of my fist, twisting my wrist a little. Billy lets the bag swing free as I take off the gloves and drop them to the boards of his back porch, the heavy bag creaking on its chain. "Let's get another drink," he says.

Inside, Billy pours bourbon and Cokes in big plastic cups. We're out of ice. The table top is sticky from earlier spills. We hear Dan halfway down the driveway, his drunken laughter joined by at least two women's. Billy pulls the curtain aside so we can watch them walk up the back steps. It's Stacey, Dan's little nightmare, and two others.

Billy looks at me and raises an eyebrow over his thick glasses. "Goddamn," he says. They can't be more than twenty.

Dan hits the heavy bag once, nearly knocking himself over, then they're all in the kitchen.

"Hello, boys," Dan says.

Stacey says, "Hi Billy. Hi Stack. Where's Lee?"

"Working," I say, hating her for mentioning my wife's name, but fixed on the other two. The one in the short skirt is just a little sleazy, in her textured tube top and teased-up dirty blond hair, but she's got a beautiful face, sculpted and tan, hard dark eyes. She smiles at me, and I swear to God, it's like I've been chosen.

"Oh," Stacey says, "this is Sharon and Kristy."

Billy and I smile. Sharon might be a great person, a fucking genius for all I know, but Kristy's something altogether different, animal-sure of her power to attract.

"Where's the beer?" Dan says, his head stuck in the refrigerator.

"We're out," Billy says. "You'll have to go to the store."

Dan nearly loses his balance as he turns toward the table. "Out?" he says. "I just bought a case."

"Get ice too," Billy says.

"Daniel," Stacey says in her crow's voice, "you have mustard on your shirt."

Dan pulls his T-shirt away from himself trying to find the offensive stain.

"Slob," Stacey says.

"Where's the fucking beer?" Dan says, and Billy says, "I told you, we're out."

Sharon, the perfectly acceptable but unsexy friend says, "Stacey, can I use the bathroom?" and Kristy says, "Me too."

"Come on," Stacey says, "it's upstairs."

When we hear their steps on the stairs, Billy says, "Who's Kristy?"

Dan's still looking for the stain on his shirt. "I don't know," he says. "Friend of Stacey's. Work."

Billy looks at me soberly, seriously. "Did you see the ass on her?"

"Looks like she wanted Stack," Dan says. "Young enough to be your sister."

"What is he talking about?" Billy asks me.

"Is there no beer in this house?"

Billy rolls his eyes.

"None," I say.

"Where have you guys been, anyway?"

"Palace," Dan says. "She's got tits too."

"Will you listen to him?" Billy says.

Dan's head floats over his shoulders as he examines the bottle of bourbon at the counter. "This stuff any good?"

"We need ice," Billy says. "Come on, you've only got fifteen minutes."

"All right already."

Dan walks to the staircase and yells up that he's going for beer.

"Daniel," Stacey shrieks down. "I think you've had enough."

He seems to study the floor, his head still swimming. "Fuck it," he says. "Who does she think she is, my mother?"

"Yes, Dan," Billy says.

"Fuck it," Dan says, the screen door slamming behind him. We watch him through the window as he bumps into the heavy bag and curses.

Billy makes fresh drinks and we move to the porch steps, Billy telling the story of the girl upstairs at Spring Street who came down one night for a light and stayed six hours, teasing. I've heard this story fifty times and never get tired of it. She wanted to dance for them. Honest to God, she started taking off her clothes. They were all drunk and she was down to her underwear and even let them touch her for a few minutes before she freaked and ran out of the place. Billy still has her bra. I've seen it.

The women's laughter bursts from the living room, Stacey's cackle loudest.

We're quiet awhile, savoring the story, then I say, "Sometimes I go crazy from wanting all these women I see."

Billy pushes the bag.

"And it just gets worse when you're married."

"Bullshit," he says. "You've got everything."

"Hey, you guys," Stacey calls from the kitchen, "Where's Daniel?"

"He'll be back," Billy says.

"Well, can we have a drink or something?"

"It's on the counter."

"I don't know how to make it."

I follow Billy inside. While he makes the drinks, I go in the little room between the kitchen and living room and put on a Sinatra album. It started as a joke a few years back but now we almost always play it this time of Friday night. I stick my head into the living room and ask Sharon and Kristy if the music's too loud; they shake their heads. Kristy smiles and says, "I love Frank," nothing necessarily sexy about that, but it's the way she says it that gets to me, like she's really saying something else, something filthy. My hands start shaking. "Wanna dance?" I say, and she says, "Sure," and walks toward me.

I am somebody else, Frank himself, possibly. I have never done anything like this. I don't know how to dance. My arm is around her and her hand is in my hand and we're shuffling around the floor, Frank singing about flying to the moon, and she's pressed up against me, the smell of her hair and perfume all around. She rubs her face against my neck and settles in closer. It's a mating dance, I'm thinking, two fit individuals of the species preparing to fulfill their biological destinies.

I am falling deeply in love as Frank demands that I use my mentality, that I wake up to reality.

Don't you know you fool, he says, you never can win, but the thing is, it feels like I am winning. As we turn, I see Billy over her shoulder, standing in the doorway with a drink in each hand, watching.

"Just doing a little dancing," I scream over the music.

Kristy twists to see who I'm screaming at and then the song ends. I smile at her. "Thanks," I say. "I think your drink's ready." She smiles back. "Thank you," she says. As we disengage, her hand lingers on mine. She gives a little squeeze and I squeeze back, and then she's walking toward Billy and the drinks. I turn the music down and walk back to the porch.

"Did Stacey see that?" I say.

"I don't think so." We sit on the steps. "But you'd better be careful."

"See what?" Dan says halfway down the driveway.

We turn and watch him make his way toward us, bent under the weight of the beer and the ice and his drunk. "Nothing," Billy says.

Dan sets the beer at our feet. "You want one?" he says.

"Get that ice in here, Daniel," Stacey says through the window, "before it melts."

"Yes, dear," Dan says.

"Coming, Mummy," Billy says, and Stacey says, "Shut up, Billy."

Dan walks between us. "Back in a minute," he says, but Billy and I know they'll go to his room and start fighting.

"You wanna hit the bag?" I ask Billy.

"Nah," he says, standing. "I kind of like that Sharon, you know?"

He stops at the door and I nearly run into him. "Hey," he says, turning to face me. "Is something going to happen, here?"

I look at his drunk, sweaty face.

"I'm just saying," he says, "to think about what's happening."

"Nothing's happened," I say.

Billy holds up his hand. "I'm just saying, okay?"

"All right," I say, and Billy says, "All right then."

I flip the record while Billy freshens drinks. I don't care what he thinks. Kristy and Sharon talk in the living room about a cute guy and Stacey and Dan scream at each other upstairs, a vague rumbling through the floorboards. There is nothing suave or debonair about me, but I stick my head in the living room and say, "Would you ladies care to hear a little more Frank?" and Kristy says, "Love to." I don't even feel stupid.

When I walk in, Kristy fixes her eyes on mine. We look at each other as I walk to the loveseat and sit next to her. "How you doing?" I say, and she smiles: "How you doing?"

Billy walks in with four drinks and passes them around.

"Are you a boxer?" Sharon asks him.

Billy laughs. "That's an old roommate's bag " he says. "We just like to hit it."

Frank's telling us about when he was seventeen and how very good that year was.

Billy sits on the couch with Sharon and they whisper a little under the music. They laugh. His hand brushes her knee. Hers brushes his arm. It's as if they've known each other for years. Only better.

Kristy and I sip our drinks. "So, are you a student?" I say.

"Part-time," Kristy says. "I work with Stacey at the Hammer."

Frank's bragging about all the blue-blooded babes he fucked when he was thirty-five.

"That must be interesting."

"Wanna dance?" she says.

I follow her into the little room with the stereo. Kristy leans into me. The skin of her back is warm and flawless. Frank thinks of his life as vintage wine from fine old kegs. I run my hand over the glacial smoothness as we shuffle around the tiny space.

She breathes against my neck, hair teased up but soft brushing my cheek. I feel like I'm thirteen again, at the back of the ski club bus with Susie Devore, reaching my arm around her, knowing my life's finally going to begin, that, any minute, we're going to start kissing and never want to stop. The song ends and we continue swaying, leaning against each other, my left hand clasped in her right and my other hand massaging her perfect, tan shoulders.

Frank refers to Chicago as his kind of town. Kristy's hand moves up and down my spine. I rub her back, then slide my hand over the flimsy material of the skirt covering her ass, down to the hem, pulling it up a little, as if I do this all the time.

Frank mentions the Union Stockyards, and we start kissing, just like that, a movie kiss, her eyes a little blurry as she looks up at me looking down at her and then our mouths coming together as they were meant to do and we're kissing, brushing our lips together, hard and soft, small bites and her Coke-sweetened breath.

In another town, fifteen miles away, my wife is serving dinner, clearing tables, asking if everything's all right. She'll make over a hundred bucks tonight and I'll spend most of it. But I'm not thinking about what a pig I am, what a bastard, how I could never find another woman as good as her, as loving and kind and compassionate, because I'm exploring the inside of Kristy's mouth, her lips, and now working my hand under the waistband of her underwear so I can feel the real live skin of her ass, and she's rubbing against me, her hand on my ass as well, pulling, coaxing, demanding pressure.

I am fully outside of time, immortal at this moment when the light pops on and we both jump a little, caught, separating, practically pushing each other away. Frank's prattling on about the summer wind. Billy screams, "We need fresh drinks; you want one?"

"Sure," I say, but as I walk back to the living room to get our cups I'm thinking, What a fucking bastard. Who does he think he is? My father?

The album ends as I'm walking back to the kitchen. Loud and clear, maybe half way up the stairs Stacey screeches that she's not going to be cleaning up Dan's puke tonight. "Do you hear me, Daniel? Do you?"

"Fuuuuck you," Dan mutters farther up the stairs, and now she's pounding back toward him. "What did you say to me, Daniel? Don't you talk to me like that."

I hand Billy two empty cups and he hands me two full ones. Sharon and Kristy are on the porch. I walk out and give them the drinks, look into Kristy's face, which says she trusts me and that she wants to fuck. This stuff never happened when I was single.

Back in the kitchen, Billy says, "It's your own fucking life," and I say, "Exactly."

He wipes down the counter with an old gray rag. "There's rubbers in my top drawer."

He won't look at me.

"Asshole," he says. "Don't be doubly stupid."

I follow him to the porch. Sharon's wearing the heavy bag gloves and rapping the bag. "Here," Billy says, "I'll hold it for you."

"Is this a piece of metal in here?" she says rubbing one mitt over the palm of the other.

He nods and puts his shoulder to the bag, explaining correct stance.

Kristy stands down the steps on the other side of the bag, drinking her drink and swaying a little, watching and waiting. She's wearing sandals with strings wrapped around her perfect calves.

Sharon hits like a girl. I put my hand on her shoulder, moving her aside as I walk past. Billy won't look at me.

"Wanna walk?" I ask Kristy.

Halfway down the dirt driveway, she's got her hand in my back pocket. My arm reaches around her and I draw her close. "Hang on a second," I say when we reach the street. "I'll be right back."

And I walk right past Billy again as he holds the bag for Sharon, offering encouragement. They even have to stop as I walk by—I don't care—up to his room and the top drawer of his dresser, Stacey in the next room saying, "You fucking slob." I pull out two rubbers and walk back down, around the heavy bag again, making them stop again, Billy not looking at me again, and Kristy still waiting at the end of the dirt driveway.

We lock arms and walk.

I'm half drunk walking down a small town street with a beautiful young woman, six or seven years younger than me. We have identified each other as fit for reproduction, filled with the desire that ensures the continuation of our hopeless species.

"That Daniel really gets drunk," Kristy says, and I say, "Dan."

"Are they always like that? Screaming and fighting?"

"Yes," I say, and she says, "Why bother," and I say, "Exactly," a kind of lie—as if I understand. It's not like that for Lee and me. Never has been.

The night sounds creep louder, peepers and crickets and whatever else accounts for the buzz.

I pick up the pace, lead her through the gate toward the back of the park where the trees begin. We kiss standing in the warm night air. My hunger starts to return. Hers as well. I reach a hand under her top to feel her breast. It's just the newness of it, just that it's different, that I can create a response in her and she in me. It's difficult to breathe.

She unbuttons my shorts and slides her hand down.

We undress each other and finally fuck in the grass of the park, grunting and sweating and sighing and pushing and rubbing and moaning ourselves into each other—into something else.

When it's over, my heart beats in my ears. Then the crickets come back.

"Will you hand me my drink," she says.

Lee is vacuuming now, and men come in from the bar side of the joint to hit on her. She smiles and flirts, plays nice with them, but continues moving chairs so she can vacuum under the tables. She cashes out with the bartender, counts her money, our money, then counts it again.

Kristy and I dress.

I put my arm around her as we walk back toward Billy's place.

I know I've killed something for good, the best thing I have, but I'm already sliding my hand over Kristy's back, down to her ass again under the skirt. "I'll give you my number," she says, "huh?"

She pinches my ass.

Billy and Sharon are still on the porch, only now they sit on the steps kissing. They look at us with the same sex-blurred eyes we must be wearing. "We went for a walk," I say.

"Beautiful night," Kristy says, and Sharon says, "Beautiful."

Lee's opening the front door, talking baby talk to the dog. She lets him out and checks the machine for messages. Wired from work, she pours a drink and plans to wait up for me.

I push the heavy bag and it creaks on its chain, nearly hitting Billy and Sharon.

"Knock it off," Billy says.

"Did you like hitting it?" I say to Sharon.

"It seems kind of stupid," she says.

I look at Kristy and want her again. "I gotta go."

"See ya," Billy says.

Kristy walks me to the car. "You got any paper?"

I rifle through the glove compartment and pull out a scrap of paper and a pen. She writes her number down.

We kiss again, but it's different now, controlled, polite, domestic. "Call me," she says. I pull out of the driveway and head for home, her number folded in my wallet. I'll never see her again. I say it out loud in the car: "I'll never see you again." It's a lie. The trees form a tunnel over our little street, under the moon. Lee pours another drink, waiting. I'll get used to lying.

Glazed

Stan got the doughnuts at six, ate four, and left two for Audrey. She finished her napoleon at ten-fifteen and said, "Don't think about that glazed, Stan."

A fly perched on the doughnut, rubbing its paws together, vomiting.

Stan picked up Metro and studied Saturday's crime.

Audrey brushed the travel section against the doughnut, contaminating it with newsprint. Then she put the paper down and walked to the bathroom. "Don't touch the doughnut," she said.

Her ass was enormous.

Stan took the doughnut from under the newspaper. He ran his tongue over it and put it back on the saucer. It would always come down to this last glazed hardening until evening, when she'd take one bite, declare it stale, and throw it away.

The waste was appalling.

"I'm just saying," Audrey said, "that if Jack and Karen come through we should see them."

She stood over the doughnut.

"What?" Stan said.

"You like Jack," Audrey said. She was rubbing her hands with lotion that would spoil the glazing.

"Audrey," Stan said. "Nobody likes Jack."

Audrey sat. "We never do anything," she said.

"If you don't eat that doughnut in five seconds," Stan said, "I will."

"Don't touch it," Audrey said.

"Fine," Stan said. "Have the doughnut."

"I will," Audrey said.

He reached for it.

She clamped her hand over his and the doughnut.

"Don't do it," she hissed.

He squeezed the doughnut, cake coming up through his fingers, into her palm.

They looked at each other, at the doughnut in their fists, at each other. Stan kept squeezing.

Audrey flushed. "Jesus, Stan," she said.

"I know," he said. "Come here."

She kept her hand over his and the doughnut smeared between them as she stood and opened her bathrobe. "I mean, is this crazy?"

Maybe it was crazy. But what difference did that make now? On Sunday morning. In broad daylight and everything.

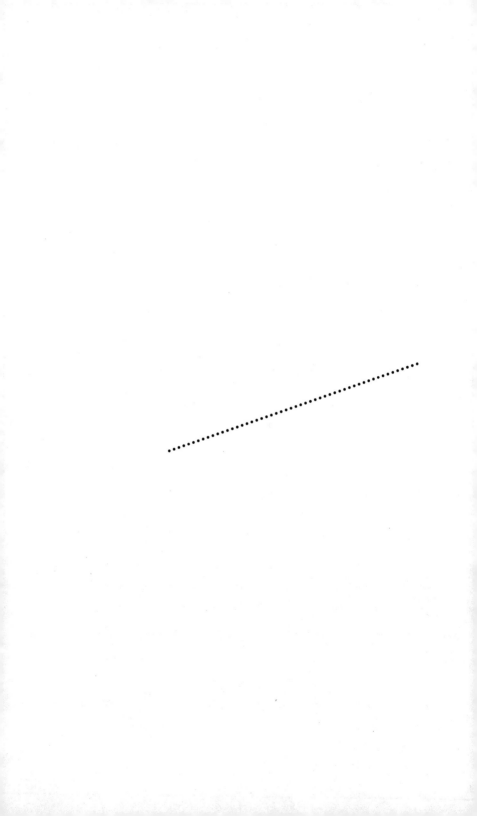

Austin

Jesus died for somebody's sins, Nikki thinks, but not mine, Patti Smith's lyrics, Patti Smith's words echoing in the silence as Nikki calms herself with a joint at the kitchen table and waits for the police to arrive, or whoever's going to come for her after what she's done to Cash, what Cash has done to himself, Cash gone ten minutes now—bleeding out the door—and it probably matters if the knife hit an organ, Nikki not sure where most organs are in a body, not knowing, except for heart and lungs, which organs might make her a killer.

But it's not as if the knife was smeared with syrupy blood as it would have been from a liver hit. And no way is he going to the cops. He'll come after her himself, if he's alive, with a gun, which is why she'd better get back to the Top Hat. She doesn't know if she can stand to see Melanie hanging on Daryl though, or worse, Daryl shrugging Melanie off and walking toward Nikki, the root of all her problems, Daryl. The root. And the more she thinks about it, the more she thinks she must have stabbed Cash in the ass. There's no blood dripping from her bedroom to the front door, hardly any blood on her sheets in the washing machine downstairs.

In the bathroom mirror, a bruise comes up purple around her left eye, a dribble of dried blood traced down her cheek from a cut where his ring must have hit. She doesn't remember pulling the knife out of him or flying to her feet as he scrambled; she found herself standing on her bed, shaking, the knife cocked close to her ear, as Cash grabbed his pants and limp-ran out of the room.

She dabs at her cheek, wondering how he got into the apartment. She was so stupid, groggy, half-drunk, asleep, she thought it was Daryl behind her—that Melanie was gone to Dallas like last weekend and Nikki and Daryl were alone in her room again, two days alone in her room, a swirl of thought occupying a second of consciousness before she knew it was Cash by his wheezing, Nikki's body going rigid as she woke.

He wrapped his hands around her throat.

"Wait," she said, her hands over his hands choking her. "Let me—"

Her words were bubbles.

Cash kept strangling as she rolled onto her back.

Her mattress sat on the floor, her jeans in a pile next to it.

The smell from his mouth was whiskey and onions, rotten meat. "You can't hide forever," he grunted, Nikki fumbling through her jeans for her knife. "Pretending you didn't want this at the Top Hat." He pushed his thumbs against her windpipe as he fucked her. "But your eyes telling another story. Your heart—" Nikki wrapped her arms around him, her forearms against his back as her hands opened the blade—"telling the same story," and she raised her knife and stabbed the fucker.

And then he was gone.

But he's somewhere. Maybe at the hospital. Maybe bleeding into the basement couch down at Duval. Maybe outside waiting. She only went to the Top Hat tonight to prove she could be in the same room with Daryl and feel nothing, but Cash chased her away, which would have been fine if he hadn't found her, if she hadn't stabbed him. If he hadn't raped her. If that's what you want to call it. Nikki takes her money from under the closet floorboard, deciding it doesn't count as rape if you've fucked the guy before. Jesus died for somebody's sin, she thinks, then notices Cash's Scratch Acid T-shirt on the floor. She wipes her knife on it and walks out the door, thinking: but not mine.

The tattooed bouncer in front of the Top Hat waves her in without bothering to check her ID, Melanie's driver's license, replaced at the DMV the day Nikki got off the bus in Austin six months ago. She walks up the narrow wooden staircase. Layers of band flyers and publicity photos peel from the walls on either side, the roar of the Shit Stains nearly shaking the building to pieces, "Glandular," or "Prostate Massage," Nikki never able to tell those songs apart. Upstairs, sweating bodies twist and slam through the haze of smoke, the stink of beer and sweat and perfume.

She snakes her way to the bar in back, almost gagging, knowing Melanie will be up front adoring Daryl. It's not Melanie's fault he ignores her. It's not Nikki's fault either. Up onstage, way across the room, Tammy the go-go girl shimmies in a short skirt and high white boots as Daryl screams the lyrics to "Bludgeon," ridiculous howling: "Hit me so I know I'm real." Bodies slam as the mosh pit expands. Nikki imagines Melanie swaying at the foot of the stage, letting Daryl know she's always available to him, one of the reasons, probably, he doesn't want her but takes her sometimes anyway. The room throbs with sound and slamming. The floor seems likely to collapse. A sculpted leather cowboy hat catches Nikki's eye, the kind Cash usually wears, but it's not Cash.

She scans the crowd, recognizing people from earlier, or from Stubb's Bar-B-Q, where she works the counter and busses tables, or from shows at Liberty Lunch or the Back Room, but mostly from parties at the big house on Duval where Nikki lived with Melanie her first five months in Austin, new bodies rotating through all the time, the core of the house being the bass player and drummer from Sludge Donkey, plus Kit, a graduate student in anthropology who sort of ran the place—Nikki not knowing what anthropology meant at first. Kit flirted with a professor named Gaylin, who was drunk at one of the parties. Kit spent last summer in Puerto Rico or Costa Rica—with Gaylin and a bunch of rich students—looking for bones. Kit took Nikki to one of her classes, where she lectured about a tribe in South America who got high on something blown in their noses, then fucked and/or killed each other. The students took notes and asked questions as if they were members of another species. As if they knew nothing about fucking and fighting and getting high. Or maybe it was Nikki who was from another species.

She gets a beer and walks through the crowd, but doesn't see Kit or Cash. Her mother's gone to jail several times, for drunk driving and drunk and disorderly, but never to prison. Not that Cash will go to the cops. Still, either him or the cops, someone's going to chase her down. Unless she kills him. Like in that Jane's Addiction song when Perry Farrell says, "Some people should die—that's just unconscious knowledge." Except in Nikki's case it's not unconscious.

The Stains blaze through a speed thrash cover of "Having my Baby," Nikki wedged against a plate window overlooking 6th Street and the party raging below. She hasn't spotted Melanie. And Daryl, as far away as he is onstage, hasn't seen her. She was probably just another fuck to him. But it's not like she wants to settle down with him and a bunch of kids somewhere, raising macrobiotic lettuce the rest of her life. There was a moment after she stabbed Cash, the lost moment when he flew off her and she was jumping upright on her mattress when, now that she thinks about it, she really could have killed him—no, really wanted to kill him—her hand wrapped around the knife handle longing to feel the push of the blade through the skin of his throat and then out and back in, fucking him to death with the knife in his throat.

"What a lovely way," Kenny the guitar player screams, "of saying how much you love me," the bodies in the audience slamming. Kit stood up to Cash, telling him more than once to get out of the house, but wherever Cash goes he always comes back, the Sludge Donkey boys wanting him around because he's the guy with the blow.

"Nikki, Nikki," someone screams in her ear, Rich, a coworker from Stubb's, holding a beer cup in each hand. "Let's dance." Even drunk off his ass, Rich is so earnest, so young or something—always helping Nikki break down at Stubb's—that she can't help but smile, giving him the approval he's so desperate for. They move away from the window, not exactly slamming but not avoiding each other either. And while she doesn't want to lead him on, she needs to figure out a place for her and Melanie to crash tonight, tomorrow night, next week, all these days and nights in front of her as she waits for Cash to attack again. She drains her cup and throws it on the floor, slams against Rich until the lights come up bright the second the Shit Stains finish "Smear," Top Hat staff suddenly everywhere with black garbage bags, collecting beer cups, full or not, saying, "Drink up, come on, everybody out."

"There's a party at the Bunker," Rich yells, Nikki surprised he knows the name of the Shit Stains' house on 38th, that he knows there's a party there when Nikki herself doesn't know.

"I have to find my cousin," she says, leading him up front. She doesn't want to use Rich as protection, and since he only weighs about one-fifty and is far too nice to be any good in a fight, the idea seems preposterous. She sees Melanie at the edge of the stage as the Shit Stains break down. It's Daryl he'll protect her from, she realizes, and walking through the split beer cups and cigarette butts littering the floor, she can tell the moment Daryl must see her, because it's the same moment Melanie turns, looking for the object of his attention, Melanie eyeballing Nikki before she smiles. "I thought you left," she yells, walking toward them, then: "What happened to your eye?"

She touches Nikki's face.

"Oh," Nikki says. She's forgotten she's a battered woman. "Some asshole slammed me with an elbow."

"I saw him," Melanie says, leaning close. "So you don't—"

She reaches for Nikki's face again, Nikki jerking away.

"Is that why you left?"

Nikki's aware of Daryl somewhere onstage behind Melanie.

"There's a party at the Bunker," Melanie says, turning toward the stage.

Kenny, the Shit Stains' guitar player yells, "Hey, Nikki; I didn't see you tonight."

Nikki sees Daryl at the edge of her vision. "I was here," she says. "In back," and Kenny says, "You're supposed to be up front," and Nikki says, "Next time," then looks at Melanie, who's watching her.

Nikki looks at the floor, wondering if Cash will shoot them both at the Bunker tonight, wondering if he's dead somewhere, bled out on a dirty mattress.

The Bunker is packed, members of the Stains and Sludge Donkey playing in the living room, a keg in the kitchen, a keg out back by the driveway, Nikki sticking with Rich to let Daryl know she's unavailable, but she hasn't even seen Daryl, and Melanie won't leave her side, Melanie treating her like the infant she's apparently become. It was a bad idea to come here where she'll see Daryl, where people keep mentioning her black eye, calling her Tyson or Rocky, everybody so fucking funny. And it's not like it hurts that much, just that it seems connected to last weekend, Cash's fist attached to Melanie's arm, pummeling Nikki for surrendering like that, but, God, if Nikki could just have Daryl, if Melanie would just get real and give up, but Nikki's such a goddamn liar because it wasn't surrender. She called him. She invited him over knowing from the minute Melanie introduced them at the Back Room months ago what would happen between them, and not just fucking. Fucking, yes. But not just fucking. Everything else, too, whatever that could be. Just everything. She doesn't want to look at Daryl. Wants nothing more than to look at him. Hopes she'll never see him again.

"I'm just tired," she says, when Melanie asks what's wrong.

They've settled on the packed dirt by the driveway, Melanie watching the back door. The music's almost as loud as inside.

"Want a blast?" Rich says, handing her a bullet of blow.

"What are they playing?" Melanie says. "Is that 'Stepping Stone'?"

Nikki can hear Daryl's voice. "You should go see," she says. "We're fine alone," and Rich looks at her as if she's issued an invitation. Shit. She doesn't want to use him any more than she has to.

"Maybe for a minute," Melanie says, standing.

Nikki takes a hit of coke as Melanie walks away.

"There's more where that came from," Rich says, and now Nikki hates him.

He does a blast, repulsive snorting noises. Nikki lights a cigarette. It occurs to her that Rich probably got the blow from Cash, a sick thought, Cash's blow in her blood through Rich. She feels like a fuck bag. But she's not going to run, not going to take off again. Cash can kill her here in Austin. Or she'll kill him and go to prison. Whichever.

She never should have slept with him in the first place. But how was she supposed to know that when the first few times just happened after parties at Duval? When he didn't turn psycho for months? When he wasn't even around much? Maybe she did string him along—before she met Daryl—finding him on the basement couch more than once and bringing him to her room. That didn't give him the right to bust through her bedroom door, though, or climb into her window at night, into her bed, making Nikki a hysterical bitch, Kit running in with a baseball bat more than once to drive him away.

"You can't just turn love on and off," he said the last time at Duval, weeks ago, waking her with his hand over her mouth as she thrashed against him. He pushed against her ass, his other hand squeezing her throat.

She felt like she was drowning, her thrashing making him tighten his hold.

"Lay still and listen," he said. And she did lie still, because he was killing her. "I won't be used like that," he said, loosening his grip as her body went slack, but keeping one hand clamped over her mouth and jaw.

She tried to bite him.

His hand tightened against her throat.

Her bedroom was becoming distorted at the edge of her vision.

Nikki went as limp as she could then, before he killed her, and kept her eyes closed tight, trying and failing to get enough air through her nose, not even thrashing when he moved his hand from her throat and wrapped his arms around her body, squeezing her to him, holding her and nothing more, Nikki just wanting it to end. Breathing. Just wanting him gone from her room. Nikki too ashamed to tell Melanie or Kit what he'd almost done to her, what he could have done and didn't. Just running, getting out, convincing Melanie to hide with her. Setting up everything that happened tonight. All of it her fault, she knows. Because of the running. Making her weaker than she can ever remember being. When she should have tracked him down and killed him.

Rich lays the back of his cupped hand on her leg, the bullet in his palm an offering. "Don't do that," she says, and Rich says, "You don't want anymore?"

"Just don't," she says.

"Sorry," Rich says, and Nikki says, "Don't be," and inside the house Daryl yells, "I—I—I—I—I'm not your stepping stone."

People dance on the driveway in front of them or talk and smoke in clusters.

Rich refills their cups at the keg between blasts of coke. It's not his fault Nikki's a bitch. She offers forty bucks for the blow, but he won't take it until she insists. "And let me get the beer this time," she says, taking his empty cup.

Standing in the keg line, she sees Kit walk down the steps in a swirly Guatemalan hippie skirt. Kit went to Berkeley, always talks about how cool the Bay Area is. But Nikki's staying in Austin, waiting to get killed. And that's the problem—that she's lost her fight, that she's running in place, running with nothing to show except fear. At least when she ran from Providence she ran with money, ran to something. She fills the cups, and when she looks up Kit's beside her.

"He was at the house yesterday," Kit says, "asking where you were," and Nikki, completely fucked up, says, "Who?" thinking, He knows goddamn good and well where I live, he was there all last weekend, and Kit says, "Who do you think? Cash," Nikki looking at her mommy-worried face, feeling stupid for not understanding before and saying, "I know. I saw him tonight," hating herself for confusing Daryl and Cash.

"Did he do this to you?" Kit says, touching Nikki's face, Nikki so tired of Melanie and Kit touching her face.

She can't talk about this anymore. To anyone. Ever. She just needs to track him down and kill him.

Back at the apartment, she leaves the door open, doesn't lock the screen. It's been a long time since she left Manchester and her mother, over a year, and she can hardly remember the feeling of possibility she first felt, doesn't know what's left for her. On the way to Providence with George, seventeen years old, forty years ago, she felt everything in front of her, but it all went to shit in just a few weeks when George disappeared. On the bus from Providence to Austin with Buckley's stolen money, the possibilities felt limitless again, another chance. Now she's stabbed some asshole she never should have slept with and doesn't want to leave or stay. Doesn't want to run. Doesn't want anything. She sits with a cup of tea in the dark living room watching the screen door, her knife open on the table in front of her. Those years in Manchester, watching her mother disintegrate, first from her shitty life, then from cancer and chemo, then, cured—before the recurrence in her other breast—and refusing to stand again, Nikki swore she would never become her.

But what has she become? A fucking groupie?

Her own disease seems to be rising, or maybe just making itself visible to her as she sits in the dark living room, catching glimpses of herself on her back while Cash or sometimes Daryl but mostly Cash fucks her again right here on the living room floor, not rape this time, but something else: Nikki on the floor under him, wrapping her fingers over his grip on the knife handle and guiding the tip of the blade to her throat.

"Can't you show me nothing but surrender?" Patti Smith says in that song about horses.

Nikki shakes her head, takes a sip of tea.

Maybe if she gets in the shower he'll kill her there.

She remembers as a ten-year-old wanting her mother to get better, all those afternoons in her mother's room when the chemo sickness was bad, watching *I Love Lucy* reruns in bed together, Nikki emptying the puke bowl and making rice pudding, hoping and praying her mother would live; and then when she got better, she became worse. But before that, it was just Nikki and her mother in bed, her mother waiting to die, so sick from the drugs as they waited and watched *I Love Lucy* and *Andy Griffith*, Nikki snuggled against her body, holding on. And then after, when she was better, was she disappointed to still be alive? Was that what fucked her up so bad?

But none of this has anything to do with her mother. It's been too easy to hate her, to blame her, to use her as a force pushing Nikki forward or away. Always the force behind her, that's what's wrong, a lie. Not that Nikki plans to forgive her, forgiveness feeling entirely irrelevant. She doesn't hate her anymore, though, not really, maybe a little, but mostly she doesn't consider her at all, which feels connected to her dream of Cash bleeding her on the living room floor, all the fight, the resistance, drained out of her.

Steps sound on the floorboards of the front porch, then move toward the other apartment, Meagan and Susan's place. Nikki jumps to her feet. She opens the screen and watches Susan unlock her door at the end of the porch. Nikki pulls her head back into the kitchen and looks at the knife in her fist.

She walks down Caswell, over on 45th, past clusters of drunk stoned students wandering home. All the time she lived at Duval she never had a key—someone was always home—but when she lets herself in the front door, no one's around. She walks upstairs to her old room, which is still empty, the mattress propped against a wall. After that first time, when he could have done it but didn't, hours later, when she woke from her coma, she wanted to kill Cash. But the feeling faded and she ran, afraid, thinking—what?—she could elude him? Tonight, standing on her bed with a knife in her hand, she wanted to kill him. But somehow she let that feeling slip away, let it turn on itself. She takes her knife from her pocket, puts it back. She walks to Kit's room, so permanent, the family photos on Kit's dresser, books and records and famous faces on the walls, people Kit told Nikki about, Anaïs Nin, Salvador Dali, Margaret Mead. Nikki opens Kit's jewelry box and finds the Mayan sun earrings. She puts them on, leaving her own earrings on the dresser. Kit never talked down to her, never made her feel stupid. Had some childish sense of justice, fighting a lost fight for the fuckups, the hopeless cases, the dead, Kit and Melanie the best people Nikki's ever known. She doesn't want to think about Daryl, doesn't want to want like that ever again. She has to stop losing herself.

She lies on Kit's double bed, her head on Kit's pillow. She imagines wanting to uncover bones in Guatemala, wanting to teach people what bones mean.

It seems ridiculous.

She lifts herself from Kit's bed and wanders downstairs, through the living room, the kitchen, walks down the creaking wooden steps to the basement, the air thick with mildew. When she turns, he's on the couch against the far wall where she thought he would be, or someone is, a body stretched under a blanket, dimly illuminated by the light at the top of the stairs. She opens the knife. Her body seems to vibrate. The other body across the room is covered with an afghan somebody's dead grandmother made. Nikki can't imagine a world of knitting grandmothers. The body moves and wheezes. She inches toward him. He wheezes and groans on his side, facing away from her. She grips the knife in her fist as she crouches, lowers the tip close to his throat, her face above his, watching him, waiting.

She remembers that night in bed when Cash said you can't turn love on and off. Billie Holiday says, "You don't know what love is," her mother's record. Before she got sick, her mother always had music in the house, but after she got better and was worse than dead, the music was gone. Maybe nobody knows what love is. But Nikki loves Melanie. Kit. She loves Daryl, even though—

Cash's eyes are open, looking into Nikki's face, startling her. But he doesn't seem afraid, doesn't seem angry. Cash watches Nikki like a child in the night who doesn't know if he's asleep or awake. She has never seen him so calm. Is he calculating the movement that will save his life? He doesn't seem to be calculating anything, seems half settled into death. What kind of story would Kit make from his bones, from Nikki's bones? What kind of lies? The light from the top of the stairs shines in his pupils. Who are you? she thinks. What do you want?

She hears his wheezing as he looks at her. Maybe he's wondering the same thing, wondering who Nikki is. Maybe it's Nikki who doesn't know if she's asleep or awake. She recognizes his face, but has no idea who he is, this calm version of Cash waiting for whatever Nikki will do to him. Begging with his eyes. Or, no. Just watching. Waiting.

He clears his throat.

They look at each other.

His arms are rigid against his body.

"Are you paralyzed?" she says.

She holds the knife above his Adam's apple.

He lifts his head slightly, lowering his eyes to the knife.

"You fuck," she says. "I fucking hate you," but bringing the words into air seems to rob them of power, seems to further bleed the hatred, his glassy-eyed stare and every second passing making him less hateable still.

She puts the point of the knife against his throat.

He looks into her eyes, and she realizes how high he is.

"What'd you take?" she says.

"Percocets," he mumbles.

"How many?"

"Four, five. I don't—"

He closes his eyes. She lifts the knife from a dot of blood coming up on his neck.

"Fuckhead," she says, slapping his face. "Wake up."

His eyes pop open and droop back closed.

"I'm going to kill you," she says, but it seems that the fucker is going to sleep through his own murder, indifferent, or worse, make Nikki a tool in his suicide.

His hand rises from the afghan—a pathetic protest?—and drops.

She feels stuck, studying his limp hand, the edge of her hatred blunted and dull; she has to do something, has to take something from him, but taking his life would be giving hers away, another form of surrender. Her eyes scan the basement. Cash groans through the Percocets. She looks at his hand, then runs upstairs to the kitchen, grabbing the cutting board and Kit's cleaver, a huge roll of twine and some rags from the drawer, reminding herself what a fucker Cash is, reminding herself that he made her run, made her weak, that he raped her, poisoned her with surrender. And this is going to be for her mother too, for George, for Frank; this is going to be what she takes, her reminder, what she'll have.

Downstairs, Cash snores with his mouth open, an empty bottle of whiskey on the floor beside him. She wraps the twine around his neck, five turns, then runs the ends over the couch arm and ties them to the legs. She wraps his ankles, twenty, thirty turns of twine, then his left wrist, securing it to his twine-wrapped ankles. She doesn't want to rot in prison, doesn't want to run. She takes his right hand and lays it flat on the cutting board. All she wants is a finger. No—part of a finger, his pinky tip above the top knuckle. Something of his to keep.

She looks at his face before she takes it, and wonders who could ever love him. Who could love her. Maybe he'll never be more lovable. But, God, if love is just waiting for the knife, she doesn't want it. She doesn't know what love is, but it's not waiting for the knife.

She spreads his hand on the cutting board, holds his pinky at its base, separating it from his other fingers. She lifts the cleaver and comes down hard.

Cash jerks up howling, the twine around his neck restraining him.

Nikki puts the cleaver to his throat. "Lie back," she hisses.

Tears come from his eyes.

She doesn't know where the fingertip landed. She drops the cleaver and puts her knife against his throat. He holds his hand up. Blood runs down it and over his wrist from the pinky stub. He looks at it, looks at Nikki, and passes out. She takes a rag and applies pressure to the stub. She doesn't want him to bleed to death. Two rags soak before the blood starts to clot. She cuts strips and bandages his pinky, cuts the twine wrapped round his neck. The fingertip sits on a braided rug a few feet from the couch. She examines it, then wraps it in a rag and puts it in her pocket. She'll carry it with her until she doesn't need it anymore. She walks upstairs, aware of her lungs pulling air, aware of her legs carrying her. She seems to float through the house, through the door, the soft gray light coming on over Duval, Cash's throbbing finger in her pocket, the whole world asleep around her as Nikki floats away home.

Arson

"Do you think they could tell?" Karen asked, draping a paper towel over his knee and handing him an apple. "It seemed so strange not bringing it up."

"I don't know," Robert said. A semi was climbing his ass, but he had nowhere to go, the camper in front of him slogging along and a steady stream of cars in the left lane ignoring his blinker. They hadn't talked about it in weeks.

Karen bit into her apple.

He saw the slot, between a Saturn and an El Camino, and pinched his way in, the redneck in the El Camino laying on the horn. Karen held up her middle finger without looking back.

"Careful," Robert said.

Karen turned in her seat.

"Don't look at him, for Christ's sake. Don't give him a reason to shoot."

They cleared the camper and Robert pulled back into the right lane. "Don't look when he passes."

But they both did, and when the redneck flipped them off, scowling, Robert said, "I told you not to look."

Karen said, "You looked."

"I shouldn't have."

"Yeah," Karen said. "But you did."

She laid slices of bread on the dashboard, spreading mustard over them, then slabs of cheese, sliced olives. It was nine in the morning. Robert often commented that Karen's food clock was out of sync. Olives and mustard in the morning. Waffles for dinner.

"So, do you think they could tell?" she asked again, handing him one of the sandwiches.

He took a big bite, said, "Nah. How could they?"

"That's what I thought."

The truck was moving up on him again, pushing him faster than he wanted to go. "They were the ones fighting."

"Could you believe that business with the potatoes?" She handed him the water bottle. "I mean, Jesus Christ, so the potatoes aren't ready. Big deal."

He handed the bottle back. "I know," he said. "Pinky can be like that."

"It almost felt like it wasn't really going to happen—them fighting like that, and us like old times."

He didn't say anything.

"They've always fought, though."

And we never did, Robert thought, which was what made the not-fights so interminable, so damaging as they simmered along. He remembered as a kid going over to Pinky's house for dinner and being terrified by the shouting and accusations: big Mr. DeAngelis into the wine a little, maybe telling Pinky's sister, Terri, she looked like a whore in her halter top and gooped-on eye makeup, and Terri telling him to shove it, her own father. It could last the entire meal, alliances forming around the table, Robert himself being dragged in by one family member or another, maybe the fat man saying, "What do you think, Robbie: Whore? Not a whore?"—the whole family watching and waiting for Robert's shrug before resuming the screaming. Inevitably, someone would storm from the table, crying and cursing down the long hallway of bedrooms before finally slamming a door. Sometimes it was Pinky himself, leaving Robert alone at this table of lunatics. "More bread?" Mrs. DeAngelis would ask him, handing him the basket.

Karen took the paper towel from his lap and wiped the crumbs off the dashboard. "Let's stop soon," she said. "I gotta pee."

Normally, he would have asked her to wait, explained how much time was lost by these frequent stops, but for some reason, he wasn't in such a hurry today, hanging in the right lane, dawdling up 95. He pulled off at a service area just into South Carolina, gassed up, and studied the map while Karen went to the can. "You know," he told her when she returned, "maybe we should get off 95—cut across on 26 and head up 77 to 81."

Karen shrugged.

"It's just nicer," he said, folding up the atlas and throwing it in the back seat.

"Whatever."

"You don't want to?"

"No," she said. "That's fine." She smiled a quick smile.

"You want some coffee?"

She shook her head.

He stood on line to get the coffee, a little put off by her lack of enthusiasm. Wasn't she always bitching at him to do something spontaneous? Here he had come up with a different route—a nicer, longer route, for Christ's sake, with maybe a stop in Charlottesville—and she'd practically yawned in his face. It was as if all the playfulness down in St. Augustine, the attention and affection, had been nothing more than an act for Pinky and Jill.

"That it?" the cashier asked him. "Coffee and the gas?"

He nodded, then saw the Ding-Dong display and grabbed six packages. Then six more. A dozen packages, twenty-four Ding-Dongs.

In the car, Karen was poring over the map. He threw the Ding-Dongs in back and handed her the cup of coffee, which she took without looking up. Back on the interstate, she said, "It's just that I thought we were in such a hurry. Leaving at five A.M.—'Come on, come on, we gotta go.'" This last in her deep mock-masculine voice, meant, he always thought, to make him sound like a dumb brute.

"Here," she said, handing him the coffee. "You want some?"

He took the cup and drank, handed it back.

"That was just for them," he said. "You know that. Five days is just too goddamn long. We always said that."

He focused on the road, on the lines gliding by.

"No," she said, when he was almost totally thoughtless. "It's a good idea. We'll take the long way."

He nodded. She studied the map.

"In Virginia," she said, "we could maybe take the Blue Ridge. The Skyline, maybe."

"Sure," he said. "Why not?"

She wrapped both hands around his arm, moved closer, and leaned her head on his shoulder.

Jesus Christ, he thought. What are we doing?

In Columbia a few hours later, instead of getting on 77 and heading due north, they stayed on 26, heading for 40 and Memphis, moving away from New York and home. Karen was driving when Robert pulled the bag up front and started lining up packages on the dashboard. "Oh my God," Karen said, laughing. "I can't believe you got Ding-Dongs." And he kept pulling them out of the bag.

"A dozen," he finally said, tearing open the first package.

"And we're gonna eat them all," Karen said.

He opened the second and third packages.

Halfway through the gluttony, Karen said, "What were Elvis's last words?"—an old joke between them—and when Robert, his mouth jammed full of chocolaty goodness, answered, "Somebody get me a doughnut," Ding-Dong particles flying, they both went into hysterics, Karen laughing so hard she finally had to pull over until the seizure passed.

"Oh, my God," she said, wiping tears from her eyes. "Lovable sweaty old porcine Elvis."

And it started again.

"The pill-addled, mother-loving, gelatinous king."

And they couldn't stop.

"Oh, my God," Karen kept saying through the outbursts and as they started to fade.

Robert finally said, "We must go directly to Memphis," actually meaning it, opening the atlas and tracing out the route. "Look," he said. "We just stay on 26—cut over on 40."

A semi flew by, rocking the car.

"But that's the wrong way," Karen said, looking at the atlas with him. "That's way out of the way."

"We've still got four days."

"But I thought we were going to start with the lawyers."

"Oh," he said, closing the atlas and throwing it in back. "Right."

"But who cares," she said. "We can do that anytime, right?"

"Of course," he said. But why'd she have to bring it up?

"Besides, when are we going to be this close to Graceland again?"

He shook his head.

She put the car in gear and pulled back onto the highway.

"Did you hear Pinky and Jill that night?" Karen asked just south of Asheville. They'd been quiet a long time, except for comments on the scenery. "Is that why you were so horny?"

"I don't know," he said. "Yeah, I heard them."

She curled a strand of hair behind her ear. "Do you think that was fake? Jill moaning like that, squealing."

"I don't know," he said.

"I just wondered if that was some kind of act."

Thinking about it, talking about it, made him horny all over again.

"It sounded like a porn film audition. I mean, I've known her—what?—fifteen years? and I've never heard anything like that. 'Ohhhh baby. Yeah. Come on. Hmmmmm.' Like it was put on for us to hear."

Robert grunted a laugh. "I don't know," he said. "It was kind of funny." But it had sounded pretty good at the time.

They fell back to the hum of the tires.

"It seemed like a marriage-counseling thing," Karen said a few miles later. "I mean, I know they got counseling."

"They did?" Pinky had never mentioned counseling.

"Oh, yeah," Karen said. "A few years ago. I don't know how long. Maybe still."

"How come you never told me?" he asked.

"Because I knew what you would have said."

They were approaching the interchange. "Remember to get off up here at 40," Robert said. "Westbound."

Karen pulled into the right lane.

"What would I have said?"

"Will you hand me the lip stuff?"

He took Blistex from the glove compartment, uncapped it and handed it to her.

"You would have said it was stupid."

"No I wouldn't have."

"Yeah you would." She handed back the Blistex.

"I don't think it's stupid."

"What about when Jennifer went into therapy, and all that business with my mother."

"That *was* stupid."

She laughed—a sarcastic bark.

"Karen, that was totally ridiculous. All I said was that maybe your brain represses things for a reason. To protect you. Dredging up that shit and reliving it struck me as torture."

"That's the way you get rid of things." She put on the blinker and started gliding onto the exit ramp.

"And, besides, I didn't know Pinky and Jill were having so many problems that they needed counseling."

"Jill said they weren't communicating—in bed or otherwise."

He didn't know if he wanted to hear this. And if Karen knew all this about Pinky and Jill, what did Jill know about him?

"Just not communicating at all."

"What does that mean?" he asked her. "They weren't talking to each other?"

"They weren't communicating." She was going too fast into the curve, forcing him to lean hard against the door and window to keep from being thrown across the seat and on top of her. "Slow down a little," he said. "Jesus."

"See—I can tell by your tone exactly what you think." They pulled out of the curve and into the merging lane for 40.

"No," he said. "I really want to know."

She didn't say anything.

"I do," he said, and she said, "Will you get me my sunglasses?"

He rifled through the glove compartment, found the glasses, and handed them to her. She propped them on her head.

"Pinky was more than willing," she said. "Jill brought it up one night and it scared him."

He couldn't imagine Pinky in a therapist's office "sharing" his problems with a stranger. He saw Pinky and Jill hitting each other with soft therapy bats, while the counselor, in referee stripes and a whistle, officiated.

"And he was really good. Really willing to work things out. Jill fell deeper in love with him because of how hard he tried."

"And I wouldn't—is that it?"

"Oh, stop it. I didn't say that."

"But if it worked so well for them, and you knew about it, how come you never suggested it for us?"

She fixed him with her eyes, a long look.

"Watch the road," he said.

She turned her head. "Because I knew what you would have said."

"No you didn't." Blood pounded at the top of his skull, at the back of his neck.

Karen rolled her eyes. "Let's just drop it, okay? Jesus."

"Fine," Robert said. "But if you thought it was such a good idea—and never mentioned it—I don't know whose fault that is."

"I didn't think it was a good idea, because I knew it would never happen."

She pulled the glasses down over her eyes. "I'm just glad it worked out for them."

Sure you are, Robert thought. Sure.

"We should go to Gatlinburg," Karen said. "All the junky rip-off stores." She'd turned on the cheerful side after a half hour of silence. "Is that on the way?"

Robert pulled out the atlas and turned to Tennessee. "Maybe we'll stop there, huh?" They'd been driving nearly ten hours. "Get up in the morning and head to Memphis."

Karen nodded.

It seemed like a horrible idea. What had he been thinking?

She pulled off at 276.

He twisted the gas cap off and started filling the Buick. It was only a year old, and Karen hated it; she'd wanted a Honda, and for some idiotic reason, he'd insisted on this Buick. Like so many of the other quiet fights, this one seemed to have its own logic, its own inertia. You could hardly feel the road driving this stupid, powder-blue, old-man's car. It occurred to him that this was really his father's car, not his. He resolved to tell Karen that, but when she returned from the bathroom and it was his turn to go, he could see that she'd been crying. He didn't know what to say, so he walked away from her.

The men's room key was attached to a big wooden paddle. He locked the door and sat on the crapper, feeling old and worn out, like at the titty bar down in Daytona, watching Pinky hand dollar bills to an eighteen-year-old girl: such a lovely girl, such a beautiful animal, Pinky's gut stretching the fabric of his golf shirt as he paid for the illusion of infatuation, the illusion of being worthy of her attention.

He'd wanted to tell Pinky when the two of them had driven down to Daytona, but he couldn't find a way to introduce the topic. After three days in St. Augustine, what shook him most was the realization that he wouldn't be able to visit them again, or that, if he did, it wouldn't be much fun. He hadn't realized how much, after twelve years with Karen, he relied on her in social situations, even with Pinky and Jill. He'd seen the way divorced friends had fallen out of his and Karen's lives, a little uncomfortable around the couples still together, the ghost of the missing partner always hovering, the awkwardness of introducing "dates," replacements who didn't seem to fit, all that stink of failure and hurt. Visiting alone would be like being a house guest: making his bed in the morning; carefully folding his towel.

They had ridden down in Pinky's new minivan, Pinky talking about a development he was involved in on the Gulf side, somewhere north of Clearwater, but Robert couldn't concentrate because of this quiet panic about his social ineptness. Jesus, he was going to be afloat. If he could just confide in Pinky, there would surely be reassurance, but there was no way to bring it up without ruining this last visit.

Pinky pulled up to a strip mall on the outskirts of Daytona and killed the engine. "This is it," he said. "Everything occupied." There was a Mini-Mart, Style Shack, Auto World, Sunglass Hut, and Haus of Pancake. "What do you think?" Pinky asked him.

"It's hideous," Robert said. "Like all the rest."

Pinky laughed. "Gotta make a living," he said.

Robert had nothing to say.

In the titty bar, Pinky said, "Come on, give her a dollar." And when Robert finally did, he felt like a father, handing out the weekly allowance, or like one of those pricks at the pricey uptown restaurants, early forties, with their twenty-three-year-old girls. How often he and Karen had mocked the transparent nature of these transactions. Cash and status for sex. As if those were the only things that mattered.

He returned the bathroom key, then bought a pack of cigarettes, something he hadn't done in years, and walked quickly to the car.

"Here," he said, handing the cigarettes to Karen, "let's smoke these." She didn't protest, just packed them, opened them, and handed him one, then took one for herself and pushed in the lighter.

"What took you so long?" she said.

He pulled out of the gas station and headed toward the interstate. "Nothing," he said. The lighter popped out.

"What made you buy these?"

He turned onto the entrance ramp. She'd put on makeup—too much—to hide the evidence.

"Just felt like it," he said.

She handed him the lighter and they filled the car with smoke.

"We're not going to Memphis," Karen said. "Are we."

They were in the hotel bar, an elaborate affair with plants and waterfalls and skylights in the ceiling twelve floors up. "Why do you say that?" Robert said. "Of course we are."

She ran her fingers up and down the frosted stem of her martini glass. The huge, open bar smelled chlorinated.

Robert rearranged himself in his chair. "Why shouldn't we go?"

She shrugged her shrug that meant the answer was obvious.

They hadn't talked about the house, the living arrangements. Wasn't it the man's job to move into some lousy little apartment? He could move back to the city, but he didn't know if he could be as vigilant as he would have to be, always on the alert for danger.

"We lasted longer than anyone we know," Karen said.

Was she getting drunk? Her glass was only half-empty, but they hadn't eaten much.

She looked at him and smiled, leaned over her glass toward him. "We don't have to do this, you know," she said, smiling the seductive smile that always made him feel helpless. "Just because we said we were going to start things when we get back doesn't mean we have to."

He finished off his martini. "You're right," he said, smiling back. He craned his neck, looking for the waiter, then looked back to see her still smiling at him. "You want another one?"

"I mean, decisions don't have to be final."

He caught the waiter's attention and held up two fingers. She seemed to be presenting herself to him; he felt an overwhelming urge to look down the front of her dress, which he did, and when he looked back into her face, she seemed to be smiling more seductively, her eyelids low over her irises. He felt blood rush to his face.

"We can do whatever we want," she said, and she made a strange laughing sound, like a cough.

The waiter arrived with the martinis. Karen finished her first drink and handed him the glass. When the waiter walked away, Robert looked at her and saw she was still smiling at him. He laughed a little and cleared his throat. "We don't have to do anything."

"I think we should sell the house," she said, leaning closer. "Move far away, where we don't know anybody. The West Coast, maybe." She took a drink, watching him over the rim of her glass.

"Like in the beginning."

"Exactly," Karen said. "Federal witness protection program." She was getting drunk. "New identities."

He took a long drink. "What if our new identities don't like each other?" he said.

"They will," she said. "Sure they will."

"And what will they do for a living?" he asked her.

"Who gives a fuck," she said. "Organic farming. Bunch a little kids running around."

"Tractors and chickens and pigs."

"Oh my."

He watched her play with the stem of her martini glass, rubbing the ice away. "Let's go upstairs," he said, "before dinner. Take a little nap."

She smiled and finished her drink. "Let's go now."

The blaring was not the alarm clock, was far too loud, vibrating his bones, setting his teeth on edge. Why wouldn't she turn off the clock? But it was the wrong time for the clock. He opened his eyes. Pitch black in the room, and that urgent, overwhelming roar rattling the glass in the picture frames. Still cotton-headed from the martinis, the wine and brandy, halfway to a hangover, he sat up and put his hands over his ears. The glowing blue digits on the clock said 2:34. They were in a hotel.

The noise would kill him.

Then it was obvious.

He jostled her, jumped out of bed and turned on the light.

"Fire!" he shouted, looking for his pants, his wallet.

She didn't move.

He jostled her again, shook her. "Get up," he said. "It's a fire!"

She opened one bleary eye, then rolled over.

He stood over the bed shaking her. "Get up!" he shouted over the blare. "Now! It's a fire!"

The noise was so overwhelming he couldn't concentrate on finding his pants, and she was sitting on the edge of the bed, slowly pulling on her panty hose.

"Forget about those," he shouted. "Just put on your dress and find your purse."

He pulled his pants on and saw his shoes under a chair. She was still half-asleep, half-drunk, not even off the bed yet.

"Come on!" he shouted. He took her arms and pulled her out of bed, looked around and spotted her dress slung over the television, and dragged her to it. "Here," he shouted, thrusting it at her. "Put this on."

Her hands were up, covering her ears.

He grabbed her wrists and pulled her arms forward, then forced the flimsy dress into her hands. "Put it on! Now!"

The noise wouldn't stop.

The dress seemed stuck halfway over the top of her body. He yanked it down over her, shoved her high heels into her hands, and grabbed her purse from the desk. "Let's go."

"My purse," she said, turning back toward the bed.

"I have it," he shouted.

"My coat. My silk coat."

"No! We're leaving."

"Let me get my fucking coat!"

"No!"

He took her by the wrist and dragged her to the door. Two Middle Eastern men with briefcases walked briskly past as he opened it. Terrorists? Karen tripped over the threshold, and he nearly dragged her to the floor, then caught her and held her up, squeezing her wrists, hurting her probably. "We have to go!" he shouted close to her face. They followed the path of the Middle Eastern men, followed the exit arrows. Doors opened on either side of them, and people filed into line.

"Stop pulling," she shouted.

The exit signs seemed to lead them in circles. At every corner, he expected to see the stairwell, only to see another arrow. The hallway was filling with people in pajamas walking purposefully with overnight bags, suitcases and briefcases.

They aren't panicking, Robert thought. Nobody's panicking. Not yet, anyway. And when they did, he'd fight his way out, Karen thrown over his shoulder.

At the stairwell the alarm was deafening, bouncing off concrete and steel. Karen pulled away from him hard. "Come on, honey," he shouted. "We gotta go down!" People were pushing around them. She allowed herself to be pulled.

The blaring seemed viscous, a glue or Jell-O to be waded through. Six flights down and through the exit door, he finally loosened his grip on her wrist. He took her hand now and led her away from the building.

"Stop!" she said. She yanked her hand out of his grip. "I have to put on my shoes."

"Go ahead!" Robert shouted.

They sat on a low concrete wall that formed a semicircle around the patio area and faced the hotel—a good place to watch the building burn to the ground. Sirens somewhere around them blended with the noise of the alarm inside the hotel. People continued to pour out the exit door. Robert looked up at the building, but couldn't see fire or smell smoke.

"I had time to get my coat," Karen said.

"You didn't know that," Robert said. "This building's gonna burn."

No one seemed to have any information and they all told the same stories. "I was asleep, thought it was the clock." "Happened once in Atlanta—six, seven years ago."

"I wish they'd shut up," Karen said.

The sirens from the fire engines had gotten louder, then stopped abruptly. Perhaps the trucks were at the front of the hotel. The hotel alarm buzzed harmlessly now.

Karen examined her wrists, rotating her hands. Two small bruises were rising over the pulse buttons where he'd squeezed her.

"Sorry," he said. He couldn't tell if he'd been a hero or a brute.

She shrugged. "It's all right."

He kept watching for flames to dart out of the building, windows to explode, burning bodies to start falling, but there was only the low hum of the alarm.

"Maybe the car will melt," Karen said.

He looked at her, and she was smiling.

Then the buzzing stopped.

People stood, but most were silent. The hotel, they foolishly believed, wasn't going to burn after all.

"The alarm's dead," Robert said. "Wires burned out."

Karen was watching the door. When he followed her eyes, he saw a man in a gray suit walking out the exit carrying a bullhorn.

"He's gonna tell us to move back," Robert said.

The man held the bullhorn to his face and spoke into it, his voice pinched and unnatural, as if he were speaking from the bottom of a well. "False alarm, folks," he said, still moving toward them. "Just some pranksters. Go on ahead back to your rooms. Everything's fine."

People started moving toward the door, talking and laughing. The bullhorn kept drawling: "Nothing to worry about. Sorry for the inconvenience. Proceed calmly..."

Robert noticed Karen shivering and put his arm around her. They were the only ones still sitting. "I guess we should go back to bed," she said.

Neither of them moved.

The useless crowd was filing through the door.

"Come on folks," Bullhorn said, obviously addressing Karen and Robert. When she stood, he wanted to take her by the wrist and pull her back down, but he stood with her and started walking.

She took his hand and they walked a little. Then she stopped, ran her free hand through her hair, and started walking again, shaking her head, leading him and talking too fast. "That earlier business," she said, "back before—in the bar and everything ..."

The alarm had left a buzzing in his ears. He wished she'd shut up.

"I was drunk," she said, laughing. "You know, just drunk talk. Right?" Her high heels clip-clopped on the concrete—very business-like.

"Right," he said. "Of course." He felt his throat tightening, didn't trust his voice.

Bullhorn was leaning against the door, holding it open. They were the only people left outside.

"Of course, we'll still go to Memphis," she said. "If you want to."

He cleared his throat. "Of course," he said. "If we feel up to it in the morning."

Her hand was warm and dry in his. Maybe there was a card you sent out, like a change-of-address notice.

Bullhorn smiled, glanced at Karen's legs.

Robert wanted to punch him, beat him down to the concrete.

"Goodnight," the little puke said as they walked past him.

"Shut up," Karen said.

And that made it all the worse.

Cleavage

It is summer again and the breasts rise up everywhere, calling out to me, demanding my rapt, empty attention. Every woman over fifty has disappeared as the various bare portions of breasts present themselves, tops here, sides over there, a trophy set at the beach unwrapped and bronzing. Carla watches me watch and I try to restrain myself, but they are everywhere before me, and even a quick glance or a longer glance is a sign of my restraint.

It's horrible.

And women are not a united front. Some claim to hate the objectification of the female body, while others switch hips down hospital corridors or rollerblade through Central Park in muscle T-shirts, their nipples insinuating themselves through soft cotton fabric. At a cocktail party in Bridgehampton, a woman's cleavage billows out of a summer dress as she holds forth on the swinish behavior of men—how they talk to her chest; how they won't meet her eyes; how at least hers are real.

Fake or real, I think, who cares, but her audience, bosom drunk, nods and murmurs.

"Aren't all bras wonder bras?" I ask Benny, who is less infected this season.

"Please," he says, "will you stop with this already?"

At Goldfingers the night of his bachelor party, there are hundreds of them of all shapes and sizes, and at two in the morning I see in Benny's sad eyes his loss and sacrifice, no new breasts on his horizon ever.

But I'm no better off. Nobody is probably.

"They're just tits," Benny says.

This is what kills you: first pretending not to notice, then in fact not noticing—allowing them to disappear.

In Newport with my parents, we eat ice cream and watch a woman discreetly breastfeed on a bench across the square, Carla's opportunity to ask my mother if her children—meaning me—were breastfed. She is looking for evidence to point to a disorder.

My mother nods.

"How long?" Carla asks.

"About six months," my mother says.

Too long? Not long enough?

"I think it's very healthy," Carla says, "the way more women are breast-feeding in public."

"As God intended," my father says. Now that he's retired, and especially since my nephew's accident, he often mentions God's intent.

I watch them move across the square behind tube tops and T-shirts, dresses and halters—round, heavy, light and pointed, small, medium, large.

On the train back to New York, Carla won't let me touch hers.

I reach again but she slaps my hand away. "I mean it, Mark," she says.

And I am pissed. Okay, I think, I'll find someone who isn't so selfish, someone who wants to share and be shared with, but before bed she shows them to me, holding them in her hands as an offering, and I know just what an asshole I've become.

At a state park in Northern California where the redwoods meet the ocean, we are warned that the Roosevelt elk are in rut, and from our campsite we watch big bulls pound their antlers against the ground. "Do not look them in the eye," the ranger tells me. "They will charge you." I ask a few questions and the ranger explains that one powerful bull has joined two harems, with exclusive mating rites to some sixty cows. The bachelors are lining up to fight him.

Carla is not interested in this information. It's foggy and cold which means sweaters and jackets, but everyone seems to be mating happily in their tents.

Except us.

Carla is not in the mood. Carla doesn't feel like it.

In San Francisco, before camping, when Carla is still in the mood, she says, "Isn't it funny how everyone's getting married?"

She mentions my nephew's accident only to suggest that it has brought my brother and sister-in-law closer together, which is not true.

And later: "Claire and Benny seem happy."

And even though I don't say a word, Carla loses interest after that.

On our third day camping, when the sun finally comes out, we meet the brewmaster of a local brewery and his lovely wife, whose nipples assert themselves throughout the afternoon. He has cases of ale, lager, porter, and stout, and I have some skunky California bud. We drink and smoke while the elk bang their complicated antlers against rocks, and the brewer's wife's nipples starve me.

Carla goes to bed early, but when I crawl into the tent hours later, she says, "You're like a dog. You could at least try not to stare."

"I am like a dog," I say, "and I do try."

After a long silence, Carla says, "No you don't."

The camping brochure has warned that bears are attracted to menstruating women; the ranger told me two people were mauled in June, closing the park for three weeks. It is only our personal safety I have in mind when I ask Carla if she has her period.

"What does my period have to do with anything?" she asks

"The bears," I say.

"No, Mark," she says, "I don't have my fucking period," and she rolls over.

"I'm just asking," I say, but even as I try to mollify her, I'm thinking of the brewer's wife's nipples.

"After three years," Carla says on the drive back to San Francisco and the airport, "it's not unreasonable to talk about the future."

I see my father in a sweater instead of a suit, cultivating hobbies, somehow knowing God's intent, and I don't want to think about the future.

But back in New York, the future lies under our every moment together. If I can just make it to Labor Day, the breasts will go into hiding. Though they'll continue to pop up in advertisements and indoor pools, on movie and television screens, the production line churning out new sets daily.

Even at the rehab facility in Philadelphia, where my brother has been waiting five months for his son to wake up, there are beautiful inaccessible breasts attached to visitors, nurses, doctors, and dietitians.

I hate myself the most here.

In my brother's monk's cell of a room, down the hall from Steven's, there's a narrow bed, no windows, pictures of his other kids, his wife.

The whole family is taped to the walls.

I lie on my brother's bed in his darkened room and wonder if my nephew will ever recover, if any of them will, wonder what I am supposed to do.

Later, while my brother showers, I read Steven the box scores. He wears pajamas decorated with comets and rocket ships, planets and distant stars, his hair combed over the scar on his scalp where hair no longer grows. In the five months since his accident, they've had to start shaving his chin and upper lip.

I tell him about the elk in California banging their antlers against rocks. About the maulings. I don't mention the brewer's wife's nipples.

"I think he's doing better," Jim tells me at the elevator. "There's more movement, more agitation."

I nod, we hug, I leave.

At home, Carla has begun an internal memo campaign; the apartment's dark, she's out with Renee, but on the table sits a printed questionnaire to be filled out within the next week: "What do you bring to this relationship?" it asks. "What do you take? What are the strengths and weaknesses of this relationship? Where do you see yourself in five years?"

At the saloon, I show Benny the questionnaire. "I'm supposed to fill this out by Friday," I tell him. "Do you believe this?"

Benny shrugs, reads through the questions, hands me the form.

"It doesn't mean anything," he says. "Just fill it out."

Something has happened to Benny, to Carla, to everyone. Everyone knows something I don't know or has forgotten what I do know, what my nephew's lingering life in pajamas seems to suggest. I consider telling Benny that I will never forget what he has forgotten, but it's close to midnight and herds of women are arriving. Benny watches a West Coast game while I am murdered by breasts and faces, asses and eyes.

When I return to the apartment Carla is still not home. I have no idea if she'll ever come back, though she always has before.

She wakes me at three-thirty with tequila on her breath as she leans over me, running her hand through my hair. She asks about Steven.

"Not good," I say.

She pulls her shirt over her head.

I can see the miracle of her nipples through the material of her bra as she slides out of her skirt. "What happened?" she says.

"Nothing happened."

"So maybe that's not bad," she says. "You have to hope."

I know that people have to forget, but I see him once a week, with his feeding tube and slippers, see my brother, who sits by his son, reads to his son, plays music and talks to his son, waiting for him to wake up, waiting to discover how much damage has occurred, always waiting.

"Anything might happen," Carla says. "You don't know."

That's the problem, I want to tell her. Anything will happen.

She examines herself in the mirror over my dresser, her legs long and strong, such a beautiful animal.

I want to tell her we'll be okay, that nothing will ever change. I want to tell her everything is fine and always will be.

I watch her breasts rise and fall as she brushes her hair for me, the lines of her ribs against her skin.

She wants a promise no one can keep. And I don't want to know what we're capable of, good or bad, together and alone. But I promise anyway.

"In five years," I tell her, "I'll be right here with you."

She smiles at me through the mirror. "In this apartment?"

"Maybe," I say. "Or somewhere else."

"Where?" she says.

"Anywhere," I say. "France, probably."

"France?"

"Why not France?"

She puts her brush on my dresser, still watching me watch her, then unhooks her bra and slides the straps down her shoulders.

"Or outer space," I tell her. "Think of all those planets on *Star Trek*, where the temperature's perfect and there's plenty of oxygen and the aliens are beautiful and speak fluent English."

And even though she's smiling, even though we both know something good is going to happen, even though she's lifting the covers to crawl in beside me, she says, "You have to be serious about this."

We wrap ourselves around each other. "Baby," I say, "I am serious as a fucking heart attack."

And the thing of it is, I am. So is she. Everyone serious as a fucking heart attack.

American League

Skinny stupid white boys smoking joints down the Kennedy in July after graduation let-freedom-ring night on their way to drink beer and shower in Comiskey's bleachers with all the other drunk American League fans, most of them knowing where they belong or where they're from, most of them from the south or southwest sides, not so many north shore or northwest suburban boys who belong at Wrigley, but no night games at Wrigley, no shower at Wrigley, no projects outside Wrigley, now on the Ryan, not Kennedy, the roads turning into each other somewhere, Robert Taylor Homes rising east across el tracks, sinking sun making white bricks glow orange around busted out windows and You'd better not get a flat tire down there boy, Boy you'd better not get a goddamned flat tire on that darktown express, that Nairobi five hundred, stripped shells of Vegas and Plymouths bunched up against Jersey barriers for weeks on end, cops afraid to stop, no tow trucks here man, Boy you get killed down there if you got radiator trouble, miles of miles of high rise projects named after Robert Taylor, honorary housing czar, pimp, humanitarian, who knows, who cares, shadow whitey spic side by side in indiscriminate traffic hold up, everybody late for the Sox game, white boy high school hurler saying Get off, Just park, Anywhere, because he's gotta see the first pitch, heading for college soon, and then, who knows, maybe the bigs, and they crawl crawl crawl up the off ramp to an orange jumpsuited shadow flagging them into a lot six blocks north of Comiskey, three ghosts jumping out in blitzkrieg rubble, broken glass and crushed cans, pay the shadow and run past the pool hall Laundromat, where two shadow boymen offer heroin, smack, scag, white boys knowing all the cool names, years before crack, before white boys, fresh from suburban nursery school, dream of needing heroin or hookers, shrugging off shadows and running down the endless blocks toward official Comiskey lots, armed guards and razor-wire, white boys at the box office paying five dollars to red-nosed Mick ticket seller, jamming through turnstiles past Andy Frain Polack usherman and running into the bleachers to light three joints, where you can't do nothing wrong, coming downtown for the big game, not so big, no pennant race this year, drinking them fast so they don't get warm, shadow beer vendor always there with another round and gold tooth grinning, drunk by the bottom of the third and high school hurler, maybe gonna make it to the bigs after college, already shoving under showerhead in the middle of the bleachers, comes back dripping water off glasses into beers, slapping graduate friends' backs, laughing, screaming, lighting joints, ball one, strike three, seventh inning stretch sneaking up on them, before Harry Carey went to the Cubs, when Harry Carey still sold Old Style, leading fans through Take me out to the ballgame, all good American fun until the middle of the eighth when the beer runs out in the entire park, and what kind of crime is this? they can put a man on the moon and still not have enough beer for the whole goddamn game, three white boys under showerhead shoving drunk south side SlavPolIrish American League fans, and when the Sox use up the bottom of the ninth, it's out to the car in the dark, drunk-walking past razor-wire lots past pool hall Laundromat and none of the fans coming down this far, then broken brick rubble where there's only three cars left, but why's the hood up? those goddamn animals, battery gone, stereo gone, back tires gone, hurler calling Wait to white boy car owner racing away with one ghost boy following, nobody else but six long blocks down at Comiskey where they know where to park, two white boys rushing through boiling piss smells of the street, hurler way behind, when a fifteen year old crooked bumper beater LTD lurches to the curb, three shadow boys leaping out the back door in a black blur, pushing ghost boys into alley, knives out and shoving white backs against dirty brown brick, hurler invisible down the street, hiding, knives against throats like a dream, a promise, Come on shadows saying, Give us your fucking money, pulling white boys' pockets inside out but only six dollars left after all them beers, peanuts, hot dogs, beers, knives still point throats then shadows running out the alley with six dollars and four joints, whites wearing nicks on necks but blood still inside running, outsides shaking, hurler appearing and leading ghosts into pool hall Laundromat to call two shadow pigs in cruiser, caged in front, What you say he look like? mean shadow pig want to know, A funny hat white boy say, Funny hat? mean pig say, You mean a tam? Yeah a tam hurler say, What you doin here anyway? mean say, and white boys say Ballgame, and mean pig don't say nothing about Cubs or official lots and be where you belong, just grunts while nice pig tries to get more description, knows nobody be found in Robert Taylor Homes across Ryan, mean shadow pig making white boys get out the car smelling of this sour not peanut not crackerjack smell, nice pig walking whites round to heroin alley pool hall, where they call rich cracker suburban daddy, where it's all smokey, old shadows buying ghost boys beer, saying Them's just bad boys, and Ain't it a shame, watching white boys' hands shake cues over faded green felt, pretending not to smell the almost shitting ghost boy smell, but white boys still shake, chalking cues blue, expecting knives now, not to understand old man niceness when white boys smell so sour, far away as bikini-d white girls cutting through blue suburban swimming pools, and the beers coming free, and Ain't it a shame, chalking, rubbing baby powder on pink palms, losing at pool over and over, laughing too loud and never sure what's supposed to be funny, until cracker daddy Mercedes pulls up out front, quick to the car, old shadow pool players waving cracked hands, while across the Ryan fire out one window licks brick black, now behind them, Fucking A, home to their clean sheets and sugar tits to brag tomorrow against knife points carving throats, forgetting everything they never knew, to sleep pretty all day long, starched blue sheets, sweet sugar plum dreams, to wake to mama's titty milk, suckling.

Orlando

Nikki turns eighteen between Hagerstown and Cumberland, the Potomac out her window a fat black snake. She celebrates with a joint in the Greyhound's bathroom, blowing hits out the spring-hinged triangular window as the bus rattles across Maryland. When she left Providence this morning, Buckley's money was in her paraphernalia pouch at the bottom of her leather backpack, the safest place she could think of until she had to pee around New London and realized the money could be stolen. Now it's two fat rolls in the front pockets of her jeans. Thinking about the money makes her want to touch it again, smell it. She knocks the cherry from the joint out the window and stashes the roach, then pulls out Buckley's money—her money—and counts it one more time. She's still rich, still worth twenty-three hundred bucks, more than anyone she has ever known.

Out on the sleeping bus, Nikki settles into her window seat and puts on her headphones, the only other person in her row a weathered nun leaning against the opposite window asleep. Nikki calls her the smoking nun, because she lit one cigarette after another out of Baltimore as she read a hardback book called *Breathing Lessons*. At least she didn't try to make conversation. Nikki doesn't know what she'd say to a nun. Since Baltimore, she's been listening to *Life's Too Good*, by The Sugarcubes, but skipping that song "Birthday," holding it off until this moment, stoned, alone on the bus in the first minutes of finally being eighteen. Now she hits play and listens, the diesel smell around her, the Potomac—and she knows it's the Potomac because she asked the driver—still unwinding out her window, the bus and Nikki heading for Pennsylvania, Ohio, Kentucky, Tennessee, all these places she's never been, Bjork saying, "They're smoking cigars. They lie in the bathtub," the greenish light inside the bus perfect with the music and her buzz, thirty-five hours until Austin, another place she's never been, and her cousin Melanie, Nikki's whole life waiting to happen. When the song ends, she rewinds it and plays it again. And again.

"Today is a birthday. They're smoking cigars."

She wishes she had a loop tape of this song to send her to sleep in the green light of the Greyhound going west. Last night, Friday night, she was with Buckley and this chick Maya, up all night on ex, before taking the money this morning. And though it's almost impossible to believe, she only met Buckley yesterday afternoon, a nice enough guy whose drug money has allowed her to get out of Providence and spend her birthday in all these places she's never been, though each place will be inside this bus or ones like it she'll transfer to in Pittsburgh, Columbus, Nashville, and somewhere else, which, when she looks at her schedule she sees is Dallas. She hopes Buckley won't take the lost money too hard, hopes he won't get into some kind of drug trouble over it. A rich kid at a snotty art college, he probably won't suffer much. She'll pay him back with interest is what she'll do, maybe won't even spend much of it. Maybe none. Who knows what's waiting in Austin?

When she bought the first ticket in Providence sixteen hours ago, she picked Orlando because she wanted someplace warm, and figured there would be jobs at Disney World, another place she's never been, but after transferring in New York City, Nikki got the idea to call her cousin Melanie, to tell one person in the world she was alive somewhere, but also hoping Melanie would say, Why don't you come to Austin? which is exactly what Melanie did say, Nikki not caring she couldn't get a refund for the unused portion of her ticket to Orlando, just buying a new ticket and getting on a new bus going a new direction an hour after getting off the phone in Baltimore.

Luck does change—she can feel that—all these people gone from her life forever, Frank, George, Buckley, new ones, better ones, out there waiting. And she hasn't seen Melanie in two years. She rewinds the tape again, touches the money rolls in her pockets, listens to her birthday song, the whole country out her window, the smoking nun coughing and thrashing, dying across the aisle, Nikki so tired after days without sleep and wracked from the ex and all that beer, but wanting to stay up just a little longer on the best day of her life so far, wanting to remember forever the green light inside the bus, the diesel smell, the music, the money, the Potomac out her window a fat black snake.

The driver shakes her awake, saying, "Catherine," Nikki surprised he remembers the name she told him. "You have to get off here," he says. "Pittsburgh." It's three in the morning, two hours sleep leaving her worse off than if she'd stayed awake. She steps down into a bay of running, stinking busses and waits to retrieve her Shipping Container, the box they made her buy in Providence to put her plastic garbage bag into, the box making everything she owns bulky and harder to carry than the garbage bag.

Inside the terminal, people wait on orange plastic chairs attached to each other in rows under dim fluorescent lighting that makes everyone look sick, wasting. She smokes a cigarette. A drunk homeless approaches for a smoke, the stink of b.o. and liquor and shit radiating off him. She gives him one only if he promises to get away from her, to leave her alone, which he promises. Then he lights the cigarette and sits next to her.

"I got half a mind to double up on the backstretch," the homeless says. "Church. China. Like that."

Nikki moves her box and backpack to another row. She has to stay awake thirty more minutes. She puts her headphones on, takes The Sugarcubes out of her tape player, the homeless sitting next to her again, his stink all around. "You think you're better than me?" he says as she fumbles to pop the Pixies into her Walkman. She drops the tape onto the grimy tile, and as she reaches down to pick it up, the homeless says it again, only this time he grabs her arm above the elbow and holds her like that. She snaps her arm free. "Don't fucking touch me," she says, pulling her backpack onto her lap fast and opening its front pocket. She's got a Buck knife in there, a three inch lock blade. She touches it, feels people in the terminal watching them, watching her.

"Go on. Git," a black woman says, standing in front of the homeless. "Leave that girl alone."

"I don't need help," Nikki says, and the black woman says, "You don't, huh? Good for you," and the homeless says, "I got just as much—" and the black woman says, "You got nothin'; look at yourself," and the homeless says, "If the holy spirit," and the black woman says, "Get up go," and the homeless raises himself and shuffles away, mumbling.

Nikki takes her tape from the floor and pops it into the Walkman. She hits play and the Pixies start into "Bone Machine." Even though she didn't need help, even though people end up fucking you one way or another, she nods thanks to the black woman, who sits in the opposite row. The black woman nods back, but doesn't smile, doesn't seem to want anything. Some people are like that—dignified—but not many.

The music only Nikki can hear makes the bus station unreal, as if the people smoking and waiting and poor in the hollowing three a.m. light exist only for her to see, as if she's the only real one here, which, in a way, she thinks, she is. The only one that matters. And on the first line of the chorus, she can never tell if the lyric is, "Your bones got a little machine," or, and she likes this better, "Your bones got a little mush-y." She's all by herself with the music, the other people actors performing for her or part of some bigger play or movie she can't see, that she herself is part of, inside of, that she herself's the star of. The black woman across the aisle works a complicated yarn craft, knitting, crochet, needlepoint, the woman as self-contained as Nikki. As Nikki now is. Because right now—and maybe this will change—she feels free of the hatred she's wasted on George, who suddenly seems as irrelevant as the actors here in Pittsburgh, making a brief appearance in her life, then gone for good. Is it possible she's no longer angry with him for leaving her in Providence like that? She fell honest to God in love with him, ran with him from Manchester and her mother to Providence, where he disappeared less than four days later, abandoning her in a city where she knew no one. She's spent all these hours, days, weeks, some significant portion of her life, hating him for fucking her over like that, but now that she thinks about it, if it hadn't been for George getting her out of Manchester, she never would have made it on her own more than six months in Providence, never would have met Buckley and taken his money and ended up in this crazy room in Pittsburgh, waiting for the next bus, all these extras walking through their brief scene in her movie, the Pixies singing, "Your bones got a little mush-y," and she thinks, Yeah, no shit, they did, but they're okay now, realigned and strong. Holding her up just fine. And it's still her birthday and everything is still out there waiting, and even though she's wicked tired, she could not feel better. As if it's better to be in this crappy bus station in Pittsburgh than anywhere in the world. As if there are going to be places like this the rest of her life, waiting rooms she'll sit in on the verge of something. On the verge of everything.

And on the next bus, this one three hours to Columbus and another transfer, she once again has her side of the aisle to herself. She doesn't know how she could be so wired. She's slept, what, two of the last forty hours? It's like the ex is still kicking, though the last bump she did with Buckley and Maya was twenty-four hours ago, so that's impossible.

She wakes to the sound of a familiar cough, and when she cranes her neck it's the smoking nun, two rows back. The couple in front of her are moaning, making out under a blanket. Fucking people. She wakes again in Columbus, hazy daylight, gets her box and waits for the transfer to Nashville, which is supposed to be famous for Elvis or some other dead asshole everybody loves for reasons Nikki can't comprehend.

Dude gets on the bus that evening and she knows from the corner of her eye he's heading right for her. There's only a handful of seats left, one beside the smoking nun, who made the transfer in Nashville, too; she sat in the seats across the aisle again and smiled at Nikki like they were old friends, Nikki half smiling back, looking away, not wanting old friends on the bus, especially a smoking nun who seemed to be stalking her. The dude continues down the aisle until he stops at Nikki's row, waiting. She moves her backpack from the seat beside her. She's been on busses thirty hours, driven through a thousand states, can hardly believe it's the same birthday. Dude sits himself but doesn't sprawl into her space, Nikki keeping her headphones on, though her second and last set of batteries died hours ago.

She's been sleeping and dreaming all day, half dreaming when she's awake, lulled by the motion of the bus. The dude doesn't stink or try to make conversation; he's got a paperback book folded over itself in front of his face. What she's been trying to figure out in her dreams is what to do with herself in Austin, what to make herself into. She'll have to find a job, sure, and something better than washing dishes like she did in Providence. Now that she's eighteen she can get a waitressing job, which might not be great, but at least she can make some money. That's just short term, though. What she's decided, without quite knowing she's decided it until now, is that she's going to go to school to become something, maybe a music teacher, even though she doesn't play an instrument, but when she asks herself what she's interested in, what she likes, the main answer keeps being music. Maybe she'll be a reviewer, attending concerts, listening to albums, telling people what's good and what sucks. Or—and she hardly lets herself think this—she could sing in a band. She's got a list of band names she adds to when she's trying to go to sleep—Piss Factory, Popes on Dope, and Mary Got Knocked Up being her favorites. Maybe she'll finally get a guitar and learn to play.

Dude beside her pulls a cigarette from his jacket pocket, never taking his eyes from the book. He smells like soap or shampoo. He looks at Nikki, holds up his cigarette. "You mind?" he says. They're sitting in the smoking section. Nikki shakes her head, looks out the window. She'll have to get her GED, but how hard can that be? And Austin probably has some kind of college. The other thing she could do is become a chef. Four rows behind her, in the back three seats by the bathroom, a woman's been yelling at her two kids since Bowling Green, Kentucky. "Breece," she says now, "touch your sister again and I'll touch you, hear?"

Nikki doesn't have any brothers or sisters, just Melanie, who's three years older than Nikki and as good as a sister, maybe better, everything they've been through, Melanie's mom's death, Nikki's mom's life.

"That's the last warning," the woman says, and Nikki hears scuffling at the back of the bus. Dude beside her turns in his seat to look, then resettles himself and blows smoke over his paperback, shaking his head.

"Trash," he says.

Nikki watches his reflection in her window as he turns to face her.

"The way people raise their kids."

He's twenty, maybe twenty-two, with long black hair parted at the side, big square hands.

"Breece!" the woman screams as the kid runs up the aisle, "get back here," and she scrambles after him, a chunky girl in lime green stretch pants, not much older than Nikki, catches him half way up the bus, and carries him— maybe five years old in short pants and a plaid suit jacket—silently thrashing against her to their back seat. And when he says, "Bullshit," in his little boy's voice at the back of the bus, it sounds like "Booshit."

Nikki looks at the dude beside her, who's looking at her, and they laugh.

"Kid's right," Dude says.

Nikki reaches for a cigarette and lighter in her backpack.

"Man," the dude says, "if she was my mom—"

Nikki hears the south in his voice, how he says mom "mawm."

"—I'd call it bullshit too."

He smiles at her. "I'm David," he says, and Nikki says, "Catherine," glad he's not named Jimmy or Bobby Lee, surprised she cares before deciding she doesn't.

"I've got some Black Velvet here," he says, pulling a flat bottle from his jacket pocket. "We can mix it with a little Coke."

"Sure," Nikki says.

David pulls the Coke from a brown bag at his feet, opens it and drinks. "We'll drink it half way down," he says, passing it to Nikki, "then pour in the Velvet." Nikki drinks, hands the bottle back. He's got a little scar over his left cheekbone, under his eye, like a fingernail indentation, a crescent. Like he's been marked, touched by something. Otherwise, his skin is flawless. He's wearing a Ramones leather jacket but doesn't come off tough or posing. Nikki likes how fat his lips are, or not fat—fleshy. And smooth. Not all cracked up. They look like Mick Jagger's back when he was cool.

"That's what you get for riding the bus," David says.

Nikki takes the spiked Coke and drinks.

"Sea of trash," he says.

Nikki can't remember riding a bus with her mother, certainly not across country, but if they did, she knows they would have been the trash. She hands the bottle back. "Sounds snotty," she says, and he says, "Shit," tipping the whiskey with a laugh in his eyes, his grin making one deep dimple in his left cheek as he lowers the bottle and says, "Takes one to know one, right? I mean, I'm pulling for the kid."

"Maybe you should rescue him," Nikki says, taking the bottle and another drink.

"There should be somebody doing that," David says, "shouldn't there?"

Nikki shakes her head when he offers the bottle.

"You're right, though," David says. "A guy who junks his car in Nashville for bus fare home's got no business calling people trash."

"Breece!" the woman in back shouts, and the boy runs again, his suit jacket flying behind him. David raises his eyebrows, grinning, his bottom middle teeth overlapping like David Bowie's, and they burst into laughter.

"You gotta love him," he says after the mother drags the boy back to his seat. "You just gotta," and Nikki thinks he is exactly right.

"He's running away from it," he says. "From her. Damn trash having babies they can't take care of."

"Is that how it was for you?" Nikki says. "Your trashy mother chasing you down?" and David says, "A little trashy, maybe, but there's degrees to it. Don't get me wrong. I like that kid—like a beagle scratching to get out his cage."

"But his mom's just trash," Nikki says. "Not like yours."

David squints at her. "Hey," he says. "I didn't—"

"More like mine," she says, and David says, "I didn't say that," and Nikki says, "I said that," but she can't remember her mother chasing her down, except a pathetic, predictable attempt once Nikki was already gone from Manchester, her mother sending just two letters, thank God, the first forwarded by Melanie and telling Nikki she had one chance to come home, within two weeks—or stay the fuck away forever, the second coming after Christmas, this one sent to Frank's place, where Nikki was staying in a semi-permanent way. She'd sent her mother a letter with Frank's return address on the envelope, telling her she was happy and fine in Providence, going to school, meeting people, just newsy shit, a bunch of lies, the only thing ever worth giving her mother, her mother of course waving the cancer rag in Nikki's face with her reply, exactly as she'd been doing since the mastectomies, practically blaming Nikki for her sickness, or if not blaming, promising that she was Nikki's future, drunk and diseased even though the cancer had not recurred again by the magical five year mark or even now—Melanie would have told her if it had—ending that final letter by telling Nikki she prayed night and day that Nikki herself would never get the cancer that had ruined her own life, prayed day and night that Nikki could be happy, though she herself could never be now that Nikki had gone and left her sick, left her to die all alone in a dirty apartment on Spruce Street, men and boys selling drugs on the sidewalk outside her building, and even though she prayed for Nikki's happiness—Nikki not knowing where all this praying bullshit was coming from—she would never be able to forgive Nikki for—and here began a numbered list, items one through seventeen, which Nikki decided not to read, being familiar enough with her crimes against her mother. And so maybe Nikki's mother has been chasing her for years. But not anymore. She's done thinking about her, anyway, wasting herself on worry and hate.

She takes the bottle from David and pulls a long drink. "Come on," she says, "talk about something." She wants to hear his voice again, wants to forgive him for calling the fat girl trash.

"Like what?"

"Like, you know, what you do."

"About what?"

"About anything."

David tells her he works for his father repairing appliances in Little Rock—how it's only the rich people who bitch about bills—but that he wants to partner with his uncle who owns a billboard company and cleared half a million last year.

"Billboards?" Nikki says, and David says, "You know. Truck stops. Restaurants," and Nikki says, "Signs?" and David says, "I know, but he's heading for a million bucks this year. Who cares how?"

Nikki doesn't know how anyone could dream of owning billboards, unless maybe they were going to paste up pictures of fat families mooning the highway, say, or that image of Johnny Cash, sneering and flipping off America.

She's about to tell David that, about Johnny Cash, but he says, "You gotta make your money somewhere, don't you? It's just like anything else," and Nikki says, "Like being in a punk band?" and David says, "Depends on how you think about it. Maybe it's like that."

"No it's not."

"Who'd want to be in a punk band anyway?"

"You would," Nikki says. "With your Black Velvet and leather coat," and David grins and says, "Maybe a metal band," and they trade band names until David convinces Nikki he has no taste in music whatsoever. How shallow she is to judge people solely on their musical taste or lack thereof, especially when this David so clearly understands the little boy Breece at the back of the bus running from his white trash mother. And at least he has ambition. At least he wants to do something. To be something. But no, Nikki thinks, he just wants money like everyone else. She's kind of drunk. She can't tell if she feels bad for judging this David or for misjudging him, thinking when they first started talking she could maybe like him, feeling a hint of that rush she felt with George at first. But she's just tired is all, tired and stupid, thinking without even trying, without meaning to, that what? she's going to get off the bus with this guy in Little Rock and start some kind of life there in love? Not that she really thought that, but doesn't she know better than to even start down this path? Christ, she's not a kid anymore. Plus, she's got her own money now. Buckley's money, she thinks, but no, it's hers. Besides, what difference does any of this make? She's going to Austin, to Melanie.

She looks at David sitting beside her, the scar under his eye, how smooth and sort of glowing his skin is.

The little boy flies up the aisle.

"Crap dang it, Breece," the mother calls and she tears after him, carries him back thrashing against her, the boy looking right at Nikki and saying, "Booshit."

"Like the central bank," David says hours later and halfway through the second flat bottle of Black Velvet. "The federal reserve."

Nikki takes the bottle he offers, trying to pay attention after the long string of lies she's told, that her father's a musician, classically trained, her mother dead, that her roommate at Brown overdosed on sleeping pills and vodka right before Christmas and how Nikki found her body all bloated on the living room floor two days later, what a freak-out that was, to see your best friend glassy-eyed and stiff, naked, the smells in the room overwhelming, and how Kara—that was her name—haunted Nikki's dreams even now, David saying, "Jesus, that's awful," making Nikki feel bad about lying as they pulled out of Jackson, Tennessee, though for awhile it felt like singing. Without the lies, she has nothing to say and has stopped listening as well, except in snatches.

"Nobody really knows who's pulling the strings," David says. "It's like the Freemasons."

Nikki hands him the bottle, excuses herself, and walks to the bathroom, the little boy Breece and his mom and sister on the back bench seat watching her walk toward them, the mother's eyes pointing different directions, the sister, maybe three years old, perched in her lap with big eyes on Nikki and a lollypop in her mouth, lollypop smeared on her face and the front of her white dress, Breece beside them holding a stuffed dinosaur, biting his thumbnail as he watches Nikki reach for the door handle, the mom saying, "Somebody's in there," and Nikki nodding, says, "Oh," and stands in front of them facing the door waiting. She feels something on her ass, jerks her head to see Breece pull his hand back to himself. "Hey," the mother says, rapping the boy's head with her knuckles, "hands to yourself." Nikki smiles at the mother, but can't tell if she's looking at her or not. She looks up the aisle to see David twisted around watching her, feels the hand on her ass again, and jerks around, Breece looking up at his mother, saying "Sorry," as the mother raps his head again and says, "Sorry don't feed the bulldog."

Nikki moves forward, out of Breece's reach and stares at the floor. She's trying not to touch the seats, trying not to disturb other passengers, but she's drunk and the bus is wobbling. She's a little sick. She walks back to the bathroom and reaches for the door, figuring to alert the person inside that somebody's waiting, but when she lurches against the handle, it turns and the bathroom is vacant. She looks at the mother, who ignores her, then slips inside, locking the door behind her.

She sits on the toilet and breathes. Should have brought her water back with her. Touches the bumps of money in her pockets, takes out her half joint, but doesn't light it. She feels drugged, fucked up. Did that David slip her something? But no, they've been drinking from the same bottles. She pushes open the triangle window and sticks her face as close to outside air as she can. It doesn't help. Finally, she pukes in the toilet, but almost nothing comes up, and she realizes she hasn't eaten in days. That's the problem. Somebody knocks on the door. "Just a minute," she says, sitting on the toilet and breathing. Maybe she's feeling better. When she gets back to her seat David's talking to the smoking nun.

Just an hour to go until Memphis and food, but the thought of food makes her stomach lurch. David offers the bottle. She pushes it away. He resumes his conversation with the nun, something about celestial reasoning. Isn't that some kind of soup? Nikki takes a sip of water. She's going to throw up again. She concentrates on the seatback in front of her. It feels like the time she was six years old and threw up so many times in a row on New Year's Eve her mother had to take her to Elliot hospital. They were still in the house on Salmon Street, where Nikki lived the first eight years of her life, before the annual relocation from one shitty apartment to the next on Spruce or Hanover, her mother still a secretary at Velcro, an office manager she called herself, years before Melanie came to live with them, but Melanie was there that night, their mothers—twin sisters—at a party somewhere, in the bars, wherever, and Nikki started throwing up around ten o'clock, cheese doodles and orange soda and hot dogs, and felt okay for about ten minutes after, Melanie telling her she was fine, that she'd eaten too much too fast, and she wanted to believe it because they were going to stay up until midnight to watch the ball fall in Times Square, which Nikki had never seen, imagining the ball some kind of zipper handle falling and tearing the old year off the new one about to begin, time laid out flat in Times Square, the old year waiting to tear and flutter away like the page of a calendar, but then she threw up again and another time and didn't care about watching the ball fall, had to stay in the bathroom because she couldn't stop throwing up. And Melanie couldn't track down their mothers on the phone. She fed Nikki crackers and ginger ale in the bathroom, but Nikki couldn't hold anything down, kept falling asleep between throwing up, her skin burning with fever.

Melanie helped her into a cool tub, where she shivered and threw up all over herself. Melanie got her out of the tub and wrapped her in towels on the bathmat. Nikki threw up on the floor. Finally, her mother was there, picking her up and carrying her to the back seat of Aunt Patty's car, holding her as Aunt Patty drove them to the hospital. Her mother must have been drunk, but Nikki couldn't recognize it then. She threw up one last time in the emergency room lobby, before being lifted onto a gurney and wheeled into a curtained-off space where a nurse poked her with an IV needle, a doctor shining a light in her eyes, pressing on her stomach, her mother saying, "She's okay, right? Is she okay? She's okay. Is she going to be okay?" the doctor hushing her, touching Nikki's body, Nikki wondering if maybe the doctor would marry her mother.

When she woke, the first thing she noticed was the IV tube attached to her arm, running up to a clear bag on a pole over her head. Then she saw her mother slumped in a green chair beside her bed, sleeping with her mouth open a little, the most beautiful woman in the world in her violet silk blouse and black skirt, fresh-water pearls almost matching the flawless skin over her collar bones, a beautiful princess Nikki hoped she would someday become. She woke a few seconds later and smiled at Nikki. "I knew you'd be okay," she said, "didn't I?" coming to Nikki's bed to lie beside her, but now Nikki can't imagine this memory is accurate, that her mother was ever capable of waiting for Nikki to wake and be okay. The memory must be a lie she created to convince her seven or eight year old self her mother was decent and normal, the inaccurate memory now stuck with her, unquestioned all these years buried, to come back on a bus somewhere between Nashville and Memphis where Nikki is going to vomit again.

She pulls herself up, says, "I have to—" and David looks at her, the nun looks at her—the nun a turtle, some kind of reptile—and David scrambles out of his seat. She makes her way to the back of the bus with her water bottle. No one's in the bathroom this time, thank God, real or imagined. She pukes in the toilet, wonders if Breece and his mother and sister are listening. She's going to have to smoke that joint. She can't tell if she has a fever. Only a hit or two, just enough to settle her stomach. She blows four hits out the window, then drops the roach outside and takes a few sips of water. It can't be food poisoning because she hasn't eaten anything. When she gets back to her row, David stands and the nun says, "Are you okay, dear?"

"Fine," Nikki says, sliding into her seat.

"Here," the nun says, handing David something across the aisle. "Give her this."

David hands Nikki a rice cake.

"Thanks," Nikki says.

"And no more liquor," the nun says. "Okay?"

"Okay," Nikki says.

And the nun says, "No more liquor for her."

She must have slept through Memphis because she wakes with the rice cake still in her hand, damp, as they pull into Forrest City, almost eleven o'clock in Arkansas, not yet midnight in Providence, still her birthday no matter what time zone she's in. She hears the sounds of people getting on and off the bus, then they're moving again. Still drunk, exhausted, high, she doesn't feel like puking anymore, but keeps her eyes closed after squinting at her watch, the image of her mother as an object of beauty beside her hospital bed lingering. What other lies has she made of her past? She thinks of Maya and Buckley and her, the three of them in bed last night, this morning, two days ago, whenever it was, fucking on ex, how she could tell Maya and Buckley were made for each other, a sort of gauzy halo around them, but now, half drunk, half hung over, starving in a bus she's been on forever, she knows Maya and Buckley have as much chance as anyone—none. She thinks of David talking earlier about his year in Daytona framing houses, Nikki asking if he ever got down to Orlando, to Disney World, and David saying sure he did, and he could take Nikki there, too, if she wanted to go, and for Nikki to have let herself be pulled like that, by his hands or lips or scar, or whatever she thought he could promise—if even for a second, pulled like a robot, a dog, oblivious to the pulling current—scares her, makes her wonder if she has any control of herself at all. She's going to have to watch herself from now on, if she wants to—to—what? Be okay? But no, she wants to be so much more than okay, she wants to be, she wants—

She sits up in her seat and feels dizzy. David sleeps beside her, his head tilted back, face to ceiling. Across the aisle, the little boy Breece sits next to the sleeping, smoking nun, picking his nose and staring at Nikki, as if he's been waiting for her to wake. She smiles at him.

"Bitch ass," he says, almost a whisper.

"What?" Nikki says.

"Bitch ass," Breece says as quiet as the first time.

Nikki shakes her head, puts her index finger to her lips. "Don't say that."

"Shit bitch," he says.

Nikki twists around and raises herself to look back to the bench seat, but it's empty, as are most of the seats. "Where's your mother?" she whispers across David, and Breece whispers, "Shit bag."

Nikki looks back again, but the seat's still empty. She scans the other rows behind her. No sign of White Trash Mother. She stands, works herself around David, who moves his legs in his sleep, and squats in the aisle by the little boy who stares at her, picking his nose. "Hey, Breece," she says. "Where's your mother?"

"Dong," Breece says, and for the first time he smiles at her.

"Ding dong," she says. "Where's your mom?"

"Gone," Breece says.

"Gone? In the bathroom?"

"Hell in a handbag."

"Don't move," Nikki says. "And stop picking your nose."

At the back of the bus the bathroom's empty. Did the mother get off somewhere and leave the kid alone? What kind of shitbag must she be? Nikki walks up the aisle, stops by Breece and says, "I'll be right back," and makes her way forward, weaving with the motion of the bus, no sign of the mother anywhere. Is Nikki going to have to be responsible for this kid because she fucking found him, because she discovered he's been abandoned? She's going to Austin. To Melanie. The nun can take the kid. Probably already has. She's not stopping now that her life's about to start. But after the driver turns the bus around, maybe she'll sit with the kid in a depot somewhere, until the mother or someone can be tracked down. Maybe she'll take care of him while somebody finds somebody he belongs to. Not even her own shithead mother would—but then Nikki sees the mom in the third row aisle seat, the little girl's head in her lap, both of them asleep. A wave of relief washes over her, thank God, but something else too. Almost like loss. Proving how fucked up she is, how aimless. But isn't she going to Austin? Doesn't she have a plan? She stands looking down at the mother. "Nun's got the boy," a man says from the seat behind Trash Mom. "Wanted to get the baby out the smoke."

Nikki walks back down the bus and crouches by Breece, who sticks his finger in his nose the minute he sees her. "Come on, Breece," she whispers. "Let's sit in back."

Without looking, she knows he's following. Less than twelve hours to Austin, she's wide awake again, ready. She sits on the bench seat, Breece beside her, his naked leg below his shorts touching her jeans.

Breece cups her ear with his hand.

"Asswipe," he whispers, and Nikki cups his ear and whispers, "Motherfucker."

"Fuck pig," Breece whispers back.

"Cock–a–doodle–doo," Nikki says.

She's surprised to discover the smoking nun's rice cake in her hand. She breaks it in two. "Here," she says, handing Breece half. "This is my birthday cake."

Breece looks at it, looks at Nikki. "Can I eat it?' he says and Nikki says, "Of course you can. It's my birthday, isn't it? I can cry if I want to, can't I?"

"You gonna cry?" Breece asks, his big eyes roaming Nikki's face.

"Of course not," Nikki says.

Breece examines the rice cake. He take a bite and spits it on the floor. "'At tastes like old dust," he says.

"So don't eat it."

He raises himself to his knees on the seat beside her and whispers in her ear, "Big butt birthday bash," and Nikki whispers, "Thank you, Breece," and Breece whispers, "What's your name anyways?" and Nikki whispers, "Nikki," and Breece says, "Shit pile," the south in his voice making it sound like Shitpal.

"That's right," Nikki says. And she laughs.

"Shitpal," she whispers back, and Breece giggles, says it again, the bus mostly dark, humming along south, taking her farther and farther away, drunk David and the smoking nun in front of her waiting to disappear, Little Rock and then Dallas about to pop up and fall away, Nikki safe at the back of the bus with a five year old, all these miles gone behind.

Samuel Ligon

Samuel Ligon is the author of *Safe in Heaven Dead*, a novel (HarperCollins 2003). His stories have appeared in *The Quarterly, Alaska Quarterly Review, StoryQuarterly, Post Road, New Orleans Review, Keyhole, Sleepingfish, Gulf Coast, Other Voices,* and elsewhere. He teaches at Eastern Washington University's Inland Northwest Center for Writers, and is the editor of *Willow Springs*. He lives in Spokane with his wife and two children.

The Autumn House Fiction Series

Sharon Dilworth, Editor

New World Order, by Derek Green
Drift and Swerve, by Samuel Ligon ■ Fiction Prize, 2008

Design and Production

Text and cover design by Kathy Boykowycz

Text set in Boton, designed in 1986 by Albert Boton
Headings set in Frutiger, designed in 1975 by Adrian Frutiger

Printed by Thomson-Shore of Dexter, Michigan, on Natures Natural,
a 40% recycled paper